HAN M GREENBARG

Chehnuh

First published by starlighteineadhpress 2022

This novel is entirely a work of fiction. The names, characters
and incidents portrayed in it are the work of the author's
imagination. Any resemblance to actual persons, living or
dead, events or localities is entirely coincidental.

First edition

ISBN: 978-1-73-250297-0

This book was professionally typeset on Reedsy.
Find out more at reedsy.com

Contents

1

Fipley's

I'm only fifteen percent human, but I'm pretty sure I know how to blend in. Bomber jacket, plaid shirt, blue jeans, inline skates. My motorcycle helmet is on the ground. Beautiful autumn day at the gas station. Everyone should dress like this, shouldn't they?

"Wow, I'm impressed, sweetie! Your outfit actually matches today."

"Thanks, Elana," I say.

She smiles at me as she goes into the store. Elana is forty-three years old, and from what I've been told, is a mama bear to seven kids all raised right here in the mountains. Out of all the interactions I have with humans at Fipley's, hers is the kindest one. Her youngest son Albie usually accompanies her, but he is missing today. I love when he gives me vibrant stickers to put on my motorcycle helmet.

"Whaddya think, buddy?" Brad asks as he lights up a cigarette. He stands two feet shorter than me, a rat-chewed camping tent slung across his back like a shield. Every day he walks all the

1

way from the homeless shelter to offer a greeting and a smoke. I say no every time, yet he continues to repeat the semi-annoying tradition. Human beings are really stubborn. Admirable, but stubborn.

"Cigarette?"

"No, thank you," I say politely.

"Ya sure? I swear it's good. It's a good time for best friends."

He calls me his best friend. I don't call him mine. In truth, I have no friends. Only acquaintances. Brad insists that he knew me since birth, but that's impossible since I am ninety-three. He can't be older than thirty.

"All right then, buddy." He pockets the cigarettes and moseys toward the highway. "See ya tomorrow."

I don't bother waving at Brad. His mind is already on the next poor soul he's gonna target for money.

"Twelve o'five," I read off my watch, still clutching the potato chip bag to my chest.

"We've been over this, Tenny. You don't have to announce the time out loud."

I watch Cyril walk by with a precarious stack of boxes in his arms. I've given up trying to tell him how to pronounce my name. "Spoken word is better," I say. "I like saying numbers."

"Sure," he says. "But I hate numbers. Reminds me of failing math every year in school."

I smirk at his response. Cyril always gripes about math. I think it's why he refuses to touch the cash register inside the store. "Math is vital," I say. "You can still learn."

"Over my dead body," he yells back.

As far as anyone here is concerned, I'm nothing but human. A disfigured, moody, and eccentric type of human. My name is spelled T-E-I-N-E. It is Gaelic for 'fire'. Most read it on paper and pronounce it completely wrong. Cyril, for example, just calls me...

"Hey, Tenny, would ya unload the last box?"

"I'm eating my chips. I can't let them go to waste."

Other people, like Vincent the cashier, call me Chenner. The most popular nickname I hear from strangers is 'pointy ears'. That's my least favorite. For some reason, it's Elana's son Albie who is the best at getting my name right. He takes a dramatic breath between syllables. Cheh-Nuh. That's how it should be said.

"Cyril, what are they talking about?"

"Who are you looking at?" Cyril walks out of the store, glancing at me as he fetches the last box from his van.

I point to the two men guffawing and spitting on the ground near gas pump four. "Them."

"You ask me that every day, Tenny. You speak English, don't you? You should know their whole conversation."

"But what's this business about Kent being on parole?"

Cyril grunts before giving an answer. "It means he's been let out of jail as long as he stays out of trouble. Kent is Sammie's son."

"Oh." Suddenly I recognize the man leaning against the rusty red, almost-pink-from-sun-exposure, work truck. Sammie Adage comes by for gas every week. That and the lottery tickets. I still don't know what the lottery is. It just looks like sad pieces of paper.

"Ya gonna drink with us tonight?"

"I don't drink, Cyril. You know that."

"You look like a man who can hold his whiskey. At least join us for the cards."

I shake my head, lifting a chip to my mouth. "No way. Too

much profanity, and I don't have the dollars to waste in that gambling game."

"It's not gambling, Tenny."

Cyril sounds like he's about to lecture me on the rules again, so I tightly grip the chip bag in one hand and bend down to pick up my helmet with the other. I do a quick turn and roll into the store, catching the amused smile of Vincent at the register. The boy overhears everything.

12:21 PM

I peruse each of the eight aisles four times before I pick out my noontime peanut bar. I love reading the names of products. Some of the cereal boxes are covered in a layer of cobwebs, and out of habit, I wipe them clean with my sleeve so that Vincent doesn't have to. Leaving one corner of dust is unacceptable. I set down my chips and helmet to get busy wiping and blowing on product shelves. Vincent watches me, encouraging my compulsion with an inside joke. "You missed a spot right there," he says, pointing and leaning over the counter. I clean it extra vigorously, deaf to his laughter.

"I found a new one for you, Chenner," Vincent says. "Chenner!"

I look over to see him pull a brightly colored parrot mask from behind the counter. Once a month I pay him to get me a variety of plastic masks from the costume store in town. Each one has to cover my whole face.

"Cute, right?" he says.

"I'm not trying to look cute when I wear these. I'm just hiding my scars."

"Hide them from who? We've all seen them."

"I don't like seeing myself in the mirror."

"So, Chenner, do you want it or not?"

4

"Yes." I swipe it from him, immediately putting it on. I can't see out of the mask, so I rely on my other senses to find my way around.

"Don't forget your helmet. You set it back there on the floor."

I quickly turn, peeking under the mask to look back down the aisle. Chips and helmet. And the peanut bar. How could I forget the peanut bar? I glide back to grab it off the shelf.

"You know you're crazy, right?" Vincent says.

"Cyril calls me eccentric."

"Same thing."

It never occurs to me that I'm the crazy one at Fipley's. Vincent is the one who keeps an emergency stash of oil paints in his break room and claims it's all for me. Who keeps paints in a break room?

"You out of the deep blue again?" He shows me the tube of paint as I set the peanut bar on the counter.

"I am. I need it for the sky around Mama's crown of hair."

"Of course you do," he says.

I fail to detect the sarcasm in his voice. I don't do sarcasm well according to the people at Fipley's.

"You've been working on that same painting for over three months. Why's it taking so long?"

"I keep getting interrupted."

"By what?"

"Nightmares." I try to balance my motorcycle helmet against the counter's edge as I dig in my jeans pocket for the two crumpled dollars.

"Nightmares while you're awake?"

I nod.

"How's that?"

I don't know how, but even while I'm awake I can feel and

5

hear the agony of my parents and lost friends as if they were next to me.

"I think you're hallucinating, Chenner. Might be because you're old and old people have flashbacks about their childhood."

"Flashbacks? Not hallucinating?"

"Either way, man, not a good thing. Hope you can get over that."

"I'll try," I say as I skate outside and back down the road. Back toward the cabin I've spent sixty plus years in. My home.

1:18 PM

If you take a single sweeping look at the interior of my cabin, you would think nothing of who I am or the horrors I've lived through. I may be eccentric to the average person, and I would wholeheartedly agree, except that I'm much more than an eccentric, pointy-eared mountain man. I'm the sole survivor of a forgotten genocide. Evidence, for those that need it, is scattered through each room. My old slave collar. Tarnished buttons from a cell guard's uniform. Blood-stained sheets from my freedom ride in the medical car. A bent, nine-lettered metal sign propped inside the bathtub that reads: SCORIALTT.

I was part of an underground experiment between humans and Elves. The aim was to create a society void of ancient traditions, built on the shoulders of brainwashed youth. The dark leader who initiated the final gathering of children did so by killing anyone over twenty. Some memories are terribly blurred, others as clear as fresh ice cubes. I really like ice cubes.

Mama's face is vivid in my mind. That's why I am working so hard on this painting. I layer each color over and over until the canvas is several inches thick and the image of Mama is three-dimensional in my living room. I shouldn't remember her after

6

all these years, but she visits my dreams. It's eerie, sad, and wonderful. The colors that I paint with are wonderful too. There can never be enough color. Never enough blue, yellow, pink, violet. Never enough sunshine yellow.

Changing into a brown sweater and bright green windbreaker, I get to work painting a portion of sky. Windbreaker jackets are protection for when I paint and I also like the rustling sound the material makes when I move. I trade my inline skates for slippers and push the mask up on top of my head.

"Fireweid," I whisper to the image. "Your name is honored, Mama."

Fireweid and Igneart. Mama and Da. Brave and cherished.

3:21 PM

I take a break from painting to pop in a movie and heat up leftover veggie soup. I slurp it from the pot on the stove, happily breathing in the savory steam and talking to the television. "Hold his hand, love. You're a tease." I smirk as the girl on the screen acts on my order. "That's right. You like him. Three minutes and he's gonna sing you a proposal."

The VHS tapes I own are my only company on the property. I found them in a thrift shop twenty years ago. I play the same three over and over. One is a symphony with the most glorious, tear-inducing string section I've ever heard. One is a romantic comedy about an animal trainer and a screenwriter. The third is a black and white film with a classy love story. Humanity has talent in the acting arts. I certainly couldn't pretend to love someone like that.

"I told you," I say to the television. "That kiss comes with the package. You know you're gonna open it when he sees you in the white dress."

I smile at the wedding scene like always. At the rolling

credits, I set the ladle beside the pot and go to rewind the tape. Happy endings, in my opinion, deserve a repeat performance. Seconds from pushing the VCR's button, a white flash permeates the windows, and a rush of violent rain surrounds my cabin. Lightning. My least favorite element in nature. A growl of thunder clatters outside the front door, shifting my peaceful mood to outright anxiety. I hate storms.

5:32 PM

It's black as onyx outside and a strange car is sitting in front of my cabin. I wait to see if anyone comes out from the driver's side, and in exactly four minutes, a young woman emerges. She looks to be angry and scared all at once, screaming at the rain and at her car which seems to have failed her big time.

If you know me well enough, you know I never open my door to randomly check on a stranger. I just don't have that perpetual Samaritan heart. But as I watch the woman go to the backseat and take out a baby, I feel a sense of chivalrous duty that I haven't felt in a long time. The baby is wailing, the woman is a sopping, wet mess, and the car is just being useless. I go to my front door and open it. Immediately soaked.

"Need some help?" I call out. I cringe at my own voice. Obviously they need help. What else do I say?

The woman looks startled. Her hair and clothes are so wet that she looks like she's swimming underwater.

"I don't know anything about cars," I say over the thundering downpour. "But I know some people who can fix it."

She's shivering. Her baby is looking at me now too.

"You can come inside and dry off."

She stands against the car, unsure of how to respond. Glittery make-up is running down her cheeks.

My fluorescent windbreaker might prove I'm harmless, but

8

my scars might prove the opposite. I feel the plastic parrot mask sitting on top of my head and pull it down over my face. The woman backs away, moving to the other side of the car. Bad idea, I realize. I take the mask off.

"I promise I won't do anything to you."

A flash of lightning makes her jump off the ground. She sprints toward me with her baby. "This is Wander," she says. "You try anything shady with me or my daughter, and I swear I'll use my pistol on you. My dad and grandpa taught me all I need to win a fight."

I tilt my head, looking her up and down. The pistol she speaks of could be in one of very few places. Why is she wearing such a tight, fancy dress out here in the mountains?

"Agreed."

"I gotta get my bags from the trunk," she says, her voice starting to crack. She scurries back to the car. Baby Wander turns her head to stare at me over her mother's shoulder.

This woman looks nothing like Mama, but there's something about the way her voice quivers when she speaks. Mama had the same antsy, nervous talk. She was always worried that something bad would happen to destroy our family, always arguing with Da about the trouble that was coming. Mama had been right to sound nervous. But what's this young woman nervous about other than the eccentric half-elven staring without blinking at her in a raging storm?

"Thanks," she says, rushing past me through the open door.

Suddenly I'm no longer alone in my cabin. There's a woman and her baby girl in my living room. None of us say a word as I turn to close the door. I hesitate to lock it. She might see that as a threat. I leave it alone and face my guests saying the courteous thing that I hear in movies.

9

"You can sit." I gesture to the couch.

"Thanks." She sits on the edge of it, cautiously keeping her baby girl pressed against her chest. "I'm Kara."

I nod, thinking of what to say next. I don't know how to entertain people.

"What's your name?" she asks me.

I hesitate to answer. Why should I tell her my name? She won't make sense of it. She'll just make that weird, distorted face all people make when trying to pronounce it for the first time.

"Here," I say to her. I lean over the little mahogany table right next to the door and write on a scrap of paper. I hold the paper up to her to read. T-E-I-N-E. "How do you think you're supposed to pronounce that?"

Kara squints as she reads it silently and looks directly into my eyes. "Tennay?"

"Chehnuh," I say. "My name is Chehnuh."

She smiles. "How about Chen?"

2

Kara and Wander

6:19 PM

"Chen is fine," I lie. I secretly wish this Kara woman would get my name right. Maybe I should go back to using my birth name. The spelling actually matched the sound. "Do you need extra blankets?" I ask. "Any food? I can cook you a hamburger on the stove."

"No thanks," she says. "I just need to charge my phone. You have outlets?"

"Outlets?"

Kara is looking at me like I'm completely stupid. "Outlets to plug in my phone."

I think long and hard about outlets. I do know what they are, but for some reason, my brain is faltering at the moment. I've never charged any phone here. I don't have a phone. If I have any cell reception I wouldn't know it. Also, what's with everybody's phone obsession? It's like you're all born with a phone stuck to your hand.

"There," I say, pointing to the wall behind my television. "An outlet. But I don't know if you can make calls from here."

11

"It's no worries. I just need to charge it."

I watch Kara plug in her phone, baby Wander still in her arms. She returns to the couch, looking down at her bags, then toward the hall. "Can I use your bathroom to change into some dry clothes?"

"Of course," I say. "It's that door there."

She takes several pieces of clothing from one of the bags and goes into my bathroom. Far more comfortable in a stranger's house than I would be. I figure it's just part of her personality. Maybe her brain isn't functioning at the highest level. I glance down at the two elongated zipper bags. A third smaller bag has baby Wander's name stitched onto it. Kara looks like she's packed enough for a week or two. Where would she be going alone?

I realize I've been standing awkwardly this whole time and move to sit in the only other soft furniture I've got in my living room. An antique rocking chair that Vincent proudly gifted to me on my ninetieth birthday. I apparently needed a rocking chair because of my age even though I don't look old. Vincent's an odd kid.

"Thanks for helping us out." Kara comes back into the living room in a casual and probably much more comfortable outfit. Wander is squirming in her arms, clearly wanting to be on the floor.

"Your baby looks restless."

"She always wants to grab onto things." Kara kneels to the carpet, finally setting Wander down. "This little monkey can't crawl yet, but she rolls over faster than any baby I've seen."

She pulls out a few toys for Wander, setting up a colorful play mat over my depressing carpet. I actually like seeing color and baby toys in my cabin. New life is comforting.

"You must be awfully brave to walk into a random person's house," I say.

"Well actually, the truth is that I'm emotionally and mentally screwed up." Kara appears teary-eyed for a moment, watching Wander grab at the dangly mirrors attached to the play mat. "I'm a new widow. I'm trying to figure this all out as I go along. The mom thing. Single mom thing. Brave, adventurous, but kinda stupid."

I move my rocking chair closer, taking the plastic mask off the top of my head. "No," I say. "You seem like a good mother."

She smiles. "Some days are harder than others."

"Are you sure you don't want something to eat? I can cook for you."

"No, no. Don't worry about it. I have my own snacks."

I watch her dig into one of the larger zipper bags to prove her point. "You may be here awhile," I say. "It's awful outside. And I won't be able to get someone to look at your car until tomorrow."

"Well..." she looks around with a nervous, puzzled expression. "I'll do what I have to."

I try to say nothing more, but I can't help myself. The questions about Kara and Wander are driving me crazy. Why did they end up in front of my cabin?

"May I ask why you're driving through the mountains alone with a baby?"

"I was supposed to be at a friend's wedding in Nevada, but fatigue and the storm got the best of me."

"And whatever is wrong with your car."

"Yeah." She folds her arms, leaning back into the couch, ignoring the fact that the cushions are slowly sliding out from under her. "I guess we do stupid things when we grieve."

13

"I'm certain your lack of sanity is temporary," I say. "How long ago did your husband die?"

"Three months. He was military. Killed during a deployment."

"I'm sorry."

"Apologies don't fix anything." She moves to sit on the floor with Wander, giving her a crinkly plush star to drool on. "Since we're getting so personal, Chen, is there a story behind your scars?"

"A long one," I say. I watch Wander's small fingers grip the star and squeeze it, myself almost smiling at her innocent fascination of the toy. "I'm surprised you didn't say anything sooner about my face, Kara. Even I don't like to look at my own reflection."

"Appearances are second to character."

"Wise words," I say. "I would agree with that."

7:01 PM

I quickly stand up, reading the time aloud off my watch. Yes, I have company, but I need to stick to my routine. I can feel the jitters all through my arms and legs. Kara is looking at me in a curious way, most likely wondering why I'm suddenly itching to move.

"I usually do a two hour workout around this time," I say. I don't think how strange it sounds to share this with someone. I show her the face of my watch. "If you don't mind, I'll be in my room for the rest of the night."

She looks like she's about to laugh. "I understand."

"If you need anything, help yourself to my pantry and appliances. I don't have television channels, but I do have a few movies."

"You don't eat dinner?"

"Not always," I say. "Depends on my mood. But you can have anything in my kitchen. And the couch folds out into a bed."

She draws Wander in her lap and gives me a smile. "Good night, Chen. Hopefully the storm passes tomorrow."

"Hopefully," I say softly, and shuffle to my room. But I doubt it will.

9:15 PM

I lie down on the floor next to my bed, slowing my breathing after another session of core and balance exercises. I don't have windows in my room, and I don't have any fan or air conditioning. I've taught myself to sweat out through anything, using my mind as the road to peace and freedom. I try to think positive. I try to remember all the good encounters I had with everyone during the day. But I always feel like there's a shadow choking me. Even with Kara and Wander in my cabin, I still feel something ominous. A darkness that won't leave.

"Just sleep," I tell myself. "Go to sleep, Chehnuh."

My memories come to me in pieces. Sometimes in my sleep, other times when I'm awake. I often think of the village where I was born...I don't remember the name of it, but I remember the house of my parents. I had turned eight years old a month before the soldiers came. Running home from school like I did every day. Sprinting as fast as I could. I didn't know I was running into the arms of my new family. Into Scorialtt.

3

Bartie Greenfrost

Tuesday September 5th, 1933 2:50 PM

I cut through a patch of maple trees on my run home from school, timing it just right in order to beat my friends back to the village. Swirls of crackly leaves catch in the cloak I borrowed from Da. The wind is biting my face. It smells like rain.

"I win!" I call out joyfully. "I win again!"

Mama is in front of our house. Da is with her. I lift a hand to wave at them as I always do, but my arm limply drops. There are new people around them. Soldiers. Soldiers holding rifles.

"Bartie, go back!" Mama screams at me. "Go back!"

I stop running, glance over my shoulder, and then look back at my parents. What's going on?

"Bartholomew Greenfrost," a soldier says as he approaches from the road.

He knows my name. I don't know who he is.

"You must come with me."

I move away as he steps closer.

"You'll learn everything once we drive through the gate." He lunges at me, gripping my arm so hard that I think he's cracked a bone.

Okay. It'll be okay. I nod, letting him pull me away, unaware of anything except Mama and Da wailing behind me.

"Bartie! Don't take my baby!"

"Please, don't kill our boy! Please!"

The soldier lifts me into the back of a wide truck parked down the road, and I see that I'm not the only elfling in it. Nine others all look at me with fearful eyes, but I see none of my school friends among them.

"Don't look back," the soldier says.

I immediately stand up in the truck and disobey his order. A round-eared soldier with short, slick hair and thick eyebrows is aiming a rifle at Da. I hear the shot and my body jolts. The same soldier aims the rifle at Mama. Another gunshot. Her cries for me suddenly stop. She's laying on the ground.

"They'll wake up," I say out loud. I subconsciously touch the braids in my hair. "They'll wake up." And just as I sit down with the other elflings, cloak wrapped around myself, my body trembles uncontrollably. No crying. No screaming. Just silence.

I can feel the bullets. I can feel their death.

4:20 PM

The truck passes through a huge gate and jerks to a stop. Uniformed guards shout at us. Telling us to climb off the truck and get in line for processing. I don't understand what's happening. I don't know why they wanted me to come here. Male Elves and humans staring us down. They're looking at me like I've done something bad.

I quietly take note of everything going on around me in this terrible place. It feels like a prison, but I'm just a child. What have I done? What have any of us done? I watch the elflings in front of me. The ones who argue or cry to the guards are beaten up. The silent ones are treated better. I stay silent.

"Hurry up, mutts! Undress and put these clothes on!"

My clothes smell like berry juice and the jasmine from Mama's garden. I don't want to lose the scent of home. But I also don't want to be in trouble. I change into the new outfit as fast as I can, bothered to see every elfling forced to wear the same thing. We blend in too much. No colors. All the same scratchy, dull fabric on our bodies. Shirt, trousers, no shoes beyond the picture-taking wall. I hope I'm almost done with processing.

Everything happens in a fog. I feel like I'm dreaming. I feel numb.

"Stand here, Greenfrost. Face the camera."

We're forced to line up ten at a time against a cold wall. Soldiers stand in front of each of us holding a leather collar, and without explaining why, they roughly put them around our necks. I'm an animal. A captive.

I blink hard after they take my picture. My throat feels tight and I can't help but try to loosen the collar that's been forced on me. Where are the buckles? Front? Back? How did they get it on?

"Little mutt," a soldier to my left says. "Look at me, Green-frost."

I face him, forgetting the collar. It's the man who shot Da and Mama. I know no one else who has such thick, dark eyebrows. He grins down at me, dropping to one knee when I shift away from him.

"Here. You'll like this," he says.

I stare at the little white capsule he places in my hand. "Candy?" I whisper.

"Better." His grin is wide, showing gaps in his bottom teeth. "It'll make you feel brave. Like a soldier."

"Like you?"

"Like me."

My hands are trembling. I can't look at him without thinking of what he did.

"Swallow the capsule. Your heartache will go away."

I'm confused as I watch his face turn serious. "Am I bad?"

He shakes his head, nudging me to put the capsule in my mouth. "Go on. Before I take you to the cell block."

I look down at it in my hand. I can hear the terrified elflings around me. I'm thinking about surviving one whole day and walking back home. I'll find a way home. Thinking it's not real. None of this is real. I tell myself the capsule is candy, and I swallow it.

"Good boy, Greenfrost," the soldier says. "You can call me Keev. I'm gonna be your friend."

Friend? He kills people and he's my friend? I tell myself I'm just going to wake up. Keev is a good man. He didn't really shoot my parents. He's not really here. It's just a dream.

"You can call me Bartie."

Keev chuckles. "All right, Bartie Greenfrost. Friends. You and me."

"Promise?" I ask.

"Promise," he says. "Now, about your long Elf locks..." He tilts his head as he studies the complicated braids intertwined with the rest of my blond hair. "You mutts aren't forced to chop your hair, but I'd advise cutting it off."

"But Da said my hair is my warrior mane. He and I had the same braids. We were half-elven warriors together." I feel myself panic as Keev grabs my arm and leads me to another part of the building. "Wait! Keev, you said you're my friend. Don't take my warrior mane."

"Shh. Easy, Bartie. It's for your good as well as your bunk mates. I guarantee that if you keep your hair long, every flea, mite, and rat will chew it up in the cell block. Come here." He lifts me up, setting me on a metal chair that faces a tarnished wall of mirrors. "You can watch me cut it. I'll style it like mine."

"I don't want to see," I say. I turn around on the chair to face him.

"No?" He leans in, staring intensely at my eyes. "It may be the last time you see this version of Bartie Greenfrost."

"Don't show me," I say. "Please. I don't want to look."

"All right."

I don't say anything as Keev quickly scissors through my hair. I feel pieces of it falling down my back, but I don't move my eyes from his face. I'm going to wake up soon. It's just a dream. It's just a dream. It has to be.

"Now we look like brothers," he says as he puts sticky, oily stuff in my hair.

"I don't look like you."

"Just pretend. We have the same slick haircut. Same green eyes." He's grinning while combing my new short hair. He acts so proud of messing up my warrior mane.

"I'm not the same as you," I say. "I don't have brothers or sisters."

"Just pretend," he says again.

"But I'm only eight. You're a grown-up."

Keev chuckles. "Just turned twenty-six yesterday. Sometimes brothers have big age gaps."

"But you killed Da." My mouth trembles as I say the words out loud. "You killed him. Da and Mama."

"Listen to me." He lowers his voice, pulling me further into a corner. "All of this will get better. You know that capsule I gave

20

you?"

"Yes."

"It's going to help. I promise."

I nod.

"Come, Bartie. You have to go to your cell."

He moves me out of the building, leading me through a maze of shouting guards and groups of wide-eyed elflings. We're just children. Children being shot at with rifles. Children crying for their Mamas and brutally silenced with bullets and whips. The scenes of violence in this place are too much. I can't take it. I just want the nightmare to stop.

"Wake up!" I suddenly scream. I pull away from Keev, running into the path of an oncoming truck.

"Hey! Move, mutt!" the driver hollers at me. He angrily honks his horn as guards point their rifles in my direction.

"Wake up! Mama, Da, I'm coming back! Wake up!" I yell out until I vomit. Keev has his arms around my waist, lifting me as I fight him. Nothing is clear. Nothing is rational. This is madness. I'm kicking Keev, but he won't let me go.

"Quiet, Bartie," he says. "Calm down!"

"No! Take me home! Take me home! This isn't real!"

This is madness. This is pure madness.

I don't know why I'm going crazy. I'm losing my mind. I think I'm going to die here.

I think I'm going to die.

4

Pancakes and a Stalker

Tuesday November 27th, 2018 6:40 AM

I groan, rolling onto my back. The floor is hard and cold. At some point during the night I fell off the bed...probably another bad dream. A really, really intense bad dream.

Wait a minute. I smell pancakes. I don't have pancake mix. I get up in a hurry, scrambling to see what Kara is doing in my kitchen. I breathe easy when I look in the living room. Little Wander is on her play mat, babbling as she lays on her stomach. Tinkly, joyful music is coming from Kara's phone on the floor.

"I like your hair," Kara says. "Does it take you a long time to do it?"

I slowly walk past Wander, looking down at her as I run a hand over my tangled braids. Usually I undo all of it before I go to sleep. "It takes me about an hour. Depends how much energy I have."

"The braids look good even through a rough night of tossing and turning."

"How do you know I toss and turn?"

"I heard loud noises from your room." Kara flips a finished

pancake in the air and it lands on a plate already stacked with them. She looks like a well-rested woman this morning with her glowing caramel complexion and slightly annoying sing-song voice. "I had to assume it was you having a nightmare."

"Sorry." I shake my head, looking at the crumb-laden floor tiles. "I can't control that. Sometimes it happens in the daytime too."

"Nightmares in the day? Sounds like you're hallucinating."

Wow. Did she talk to Vincent? "You aren't the first to tell me that," I say.

"I hope my being here didn't cause your bad dreams, Chen."

I start to say no but rethink it. Maybe she did cause the extra turbulence in my dreams. But I don't tell her that. She's been kind.

"Want a pancake?"

I look from her confidently standing at my stove to Wander who is now chewing a puffy-paged book. They've somehow become fixtures of my cabin in less than a day. "Where did you find pancake mix? I don't have any," I say, moving past her to pour myself a mug of black coffee. "Thanks for making this too. You didn't have to."

"I did," she says and takes a bite of dry pancake. "You could've just let me sit outside in the storm all night. Breakfast is only fair."

"So, I'm guessing you just have your own pancake mix in your bags?"

She nods, laughing at herself. "It's a quirk of mine. I carry some everywhere I go." She pushes a plate of two toward me and pours syrup on them. "Here."

"Thank you." I sit on one of my yellow counter stools, coffee in hand. "I really appreciate this."

She watches me start to eat, the flecks of gold in her brown eyes appearing to sparkle in her fascination of my face.

"What?" I ask. "The scars?"

"Have your ears always been pointy?"

Here it is. Another question I've waited to come out of her mouth. I chew slowly before answering. I sip my coffee. Women are supposed to be wise, compassionate, understanding. Maybe she'll believe who I am. Who I really am. I've told Elana at Fipley's who and what I am and she just smiled, not seeming shocked at all. But maybe she was just being nice.

"Do you think my ears are natural?"

She shrugs. "Birth defect. That's totally okay. I think they look cool."

I put my fork down, listening to Wander babbling along to the music behind me. Do I even need to be this honest? No one believes me. But Kara will be on her way soon. It won't matter if she hears it and forgets me in a month. I lean over the counter and I say, "Half-elven."

She pauses in sipping her orange juice. "What?"

"Half. Elf." I tuck stray strands of hair behind my ears so she gets an unobstructed view of my Elf features. My battle scars, pointy ears...including my pointy but bent, puppy-like left ear. "I'm a half-elven," I say.

"You're not," she says.

"I am."

Kara looks past me at Wander who's now getting fussy. She turns off the stove and goes to pick her up, carrying her back toward the counter. "Chen, I've seen a lot of fantasy movies. It would be so awesome if you were really an Elf—"

"Half-elven."

"Yeah. Half-elven. But, I mean, how can you really be..."

"It's the truth. I just thought you should know, Kara."

She rocks Wander against her shoulder. "How long have you lived here?"

"Since I was twenty-nine I think."

"And how old are you now?"

"Ninety-three."

"No." Her eyes are as big as the moon. "You're joking."

"I'm ninety-three."

"You don't look anything like that."

"I know."

"Well, your genes must be magical or you got a lot of plastic surgery."

"I never got surgery on my face," I say. "I let my scars age with me, and I guess it's lucky I'm part Elf, because I still look pretty decent. Most women tell me that anyway."

"What do you do for work? You must have some job to be living here all this time."

"I sell my paintings on the highway. Made two hundred dollars last month. In fact, it's almost time for me to go out and sell another one." I look at my watch while Kara stares at me in disbelief. "Eight-twenty," I say. "Want to join me? I just sit down the road and wait for drivers to notice my art."

"It's still pouring rain," she says.

"There's a bench under the trees. I don't stay out very long."

She looks around my cabin again, seeming to be even more curious after hearing my confession. "Sure, Chen. Just as long as you help fix my car."

"I know people who can fix it. I'll take you to them when there's a break in the storm," I say. "I promise."

"Okay. Wander and I will follow you, half-elven."

I grin back at her smile. Sarcastic or not, at least she's trying to acknowledge what I am.

"Cheez," she says loudly. "You haven't smiled this whole time! You've got a cute one."

Thanks, I think silently. But I don't want to see myself. I don't want to ever see myself.

8:59 AM

The rain is coming down hard, but there is a dry space under the forest's edge. Wander is cozy in her little jacket and pacifier, sitting on her mother's lap, looking up at me in a way she hasn't before. I don't often get to see babies at Fipley's, and seeing a baby smile like that is warming to my heart.

"How old is she?"

"Five and a half months," Kara says.

"Got brown eyes like you."

"Yeah, she does. Lighter hair like her daddy though. I thought for sure she'd get my brown hair."

"You never know with genetics."

"Genetics." She echoes my word with a chuckle. "Do you even know about genetics? If you're really half-elven, I'd think you wouldn't know any modern human concepts."

"I've been here most of my life, Kara. I haven't lived anywhere else in this country, but I've met enough modern people like you to learn a thing or two about how the United States works."

"So, I'm thinking you know what the words for things are, but not the exact definitions. You don't know sarcasm, double meanings, or innuendos."

I look from my painting on its easel to Kara sitting next to me. "What's an innuendo?"

"Okay, maybe you aren't from here then."

"I'm just asking," I say. "What is it?"

"Not sure how to explain."

"Okay."

We sit quietly for awhile, watching the rain soar down around us, droplets beaten heavily in the wind. Eventually I can hear Kara sighing impatiently, and I prepare for a lengthy description of what an innuendo is.

"Chen, I have to tell you something. Probably something I should've told you last night."

"It's not an innuendo?"

"No." She almost smiles at me, but quickly sullens. "I have a stalker."

"A stalker?" I do know that word. I know it well because one of the regular customers at Fipley's claims to have one. This is not going to help my dreams at night. So much for being a good Samaritan, Chehnuh.

"I don't think my husband's death was an accident or military-related. And I know that my stalker's still following me."

"How long have you known about the stalker?"

"Well, he's an ex-boyfriend."

"How long did you date him?"

"Ten months," she says. "He showed his true colors within five months. Possessive nature, extreme jealousy, a complete control freak. He even managed to sneak into my wedding reception. My husband Anders always told me to just look the other way...to ignore him. But I worry about when he'll turn violent. And now I'm a mom and a widow. I haven't been thinking straight for awhile."

"So," I say, "this stalker won't take no for an answer."

"Exactly. One of those crazies."

I see Wander smiling at me through her pacifier, and I smile back at her, hoping to show her everything's okay. Babies are too precious for this world. They can't know the danger.

"Why haven't you talked to the police?"

"Because my stalker never physically hurt me. I've got no proof. Not to mention, his family protects his dignity. They think he is a perfect angel who can do no wrong. But I've changed my phone number three times in the last year, and he manages to get it every time and bombard my voicemail. Every time!"

I know I should pay attention to her, but when this woman talks, she gets on a roll. I can barely follow along and retain everything she's saying. Cyril once told me that a man should never ever tell a woman that she talks too much. But it's a lot of information, and I'm not sure I'm hearing half of it right.

"I'm trying not to worry about it," she says, "but I'm scared."

"So, you have a dangerous stalker and you still decide to take a road trip with your baby."

"Anders isn't coming home. You don't know what it's like to in your house smelling the scent of someone who's not there. I'm surrounded by his things and my family has to bring over meals and flowers as if that's going to make me feel better."

I hear the strained emotion in Kara's voice and I soften my own. "I'm not trying to judge."

"You are, Chen. It's all over your face."

"You're pretty and sweet," I say. "Completely vulnerable out here in the mountains with a baby."

She stands up as Wander squirms in her arms. "Look, I know this will sound weird, but would you come with me when I drive back home?"

I glance at my painting still set in its easel. "Was that your plan?" I ask. "Hire a bodyguard?"

"My stalker's always been less than a day behind me. It's asking a lot, Chen, but you've been so nice."

"I don't have a gun," I say. "It sounds like you may want a

man with weapons, and I'm not even human."

"Yes. Half-elven," she says, hesitating at the 'elven' part. "And I have my own handgun in the car. I just haven't used it in awhile...not since I went to the shooting range with Anders."

"I'm not one to get into a fight, Kara."

"You don't have to."

"But," I say, "I do know how to punch and kick. My nightly workouts keep me fit for any conflict."

Kara smiles. "Then you'll come with me?"

I nod, realizing that I'm stuck with her. "The rain has slowed. I'll take you to Fipley's and we can get your car fixed."

"Fipley's?"

"It's a gas station down the road. I know the guys there. All of them are car experts."

"Friends of yours?"

"No," I say. "I don't have any friends."

5

Cell Block 39

Tuesday September 5th, 1933 5:01 PM

My meltdown in front of the guards scares me. I'm afraid that I'm going to be beaten to death. I should have obeyed. I should have stayed calm.

"Please," I say to Keev. "I'm sorry. I'm sorry."

He shoves me against a brick wall, forcing me to look at him. I see a metal number inscribed above us. Thirty-nine. "It's all right," Keev says. "Your old life has been taken from you. Fear is a normal state."

"Please, Keev, don't hurt me. I'm sorry."

"I won't hurt you. I'm your friend."

I wipe tears from my face, doing my best to compose myself. I don't want to cry in front of anyone. "When does the capsule make me feel better?"

"Soon." He lays a firm hand on my head. "Less than an hour, Bartie, you will feel invincible. Come. Come in here." He takes me inside an airless, gloomy room and points to the nearest bunk bed. "There are no doors attached to the cells, but do not let the illusion of freedom fool you. You are not allowed out of here unless ordered to. Be wise. I don't want to find your lifeless body in the yard."

I point outside at the wide patch of mud filled with guards and soldiers. "The yard?"

"Yes." He nods. "Stay here until you are told to come out. Hear me? Stay here."

"Yes," I say. I watch him back away, his eyes focused on me until he finally turns around and disappears to the left of the cell block.

Someone loudly coughs on the bunk above mine, and I look up to see a gawky, wild-eyed elfling peering down. His grin startles me. Most of his teeth are gone. "Welcome to Scorialtt, fellow orphan."

I look at the floor.

"Cozy, huh?" he says. "Ya can share my bunk if they let ya."

"Why are we here?" I whisper.

"Ah, ya do talk. Secrets for a reason, friend. Ya and me are the archetype of half-breeds."

"Half-breeds?" I look up at him.

"That's right." He moves from the bunk to the floor, shamelessly standing barefoot in a pool of fresh blood. "Stuard. Yer name?"

"Bartie."

"Bartie. Sounds very country-elfish. What's the last name?"

"Greenfrost." I touch the collar at my neck, feeling itchy bumps forming all around my throat. "My Mama said I'm seventy-five percent Elf, fifteen percent human."

"More Elf blood. More potent." He gives a wink, dancing around me like this is all a good-natured game.

"What are you?" I ask, utterly confused. Stuard doesn't look like any elfling I would be friends with at home.

"I'm Stuard!" He holds his arms out, yelling to the dark room. "Half troublemaker! Half wild beast!"

"You do sound wild," I say. "What did we do to get in here? What's Scorialtt?"

"They'll tell ya," he says. He lowers his voice just as the raspy breath of a new guard comes up behind us. "It's a living hell."

5:29 PM

"Your cellmates, little bastards," the guard says. He takes the blindfolds off of the four elflings he has just pushed into the room. Stuard and I stand together as he announces them by their surnames. "Grass, Dooran, Mebbith, Wildshore." His eyes land on us, and I shiver at the sight of him. "Purebloods call me Cutter. I'm assigned to your block."

Cutter has frightening white-blue eyes, a mouth too big for his sharp, angular face. Pointy ears like ours. Three deep scars across his throat, almost looking as if he shouldn't still have a head. His voice sounds like a fiery underworld creature. A demon or a dragon with a wicked heart.

"Bartholomew Greenfrost," he growls at me. "Your father was a fisherman, your mother crafted longbows for the villagers. What does that make you? What is your worth?"

I say nothing.

"I hear you are a gentle one, Greenfrost. Raised to do nothing but run from war and pain." He grins in a sadistic manner, forcing me to look away. "You will be easy to break."

I don't want to upset any of the guards. I want to survive.

"Now," Cutter says to us, "you will each drink in your initiation to Scorialtt." He gives us heavy brown bottles, and lifts one of his own in a mocking gesture of camaraderie. "Drink all of it."

Stuard is the first to take a sip and immediately coughs,

spitting it onto the floor.

"Drink the whole thing!" Cutter orders.

I tilt it back, feeling fire in my throat. Fire water. That's what he's given us. We have to drink like dragons. But we're just children.

"I can't," Wildshore says. She looks to the other girl Mebbith, and they put their fire water on the floor.

"Disobedient mutts." Cutter violently swings his bottle, striking them across their faces.

I trade horrified looks with Stuard and the two other boy elflings. We manage to drink all of our fire water, but I'm hearing the girls whimpering. Cutter is backing them into the furthest wall, throwing punch after punch on their bodies. They didn't do anything to deserve this.

"Stop it!" I scream. I let my empty bottle drop, waiting for Cutter to turn around. Something inside me is wild and furious. Wild like Stuard claims to be. I've never felt this sort of anger before. Never felt this bold. "Leave the girls alone!" I say. "Don't hit girls. Never hit them." I don't sound like myself. I see Cutter turn and stare at me and I brace for what's coming.

"You're flying high, aren't you?"

I don't know what he's talking about. I don't want to know.

"Chivalrous bastard." He shoves me back out into the yard. "You've already taken some. Who gave it to you?"

"No one. Nothing." I feel the sharp eyes of the garrison on me as I crawl backward in the mud. "I have nothing."

"Was it the powder? The capsule? How did you get it?"

"I didn't." I feel myself shaking, realizing the capsule that Keev gave me is stripping me of all self-control. I want to lash out.

"It was Keev, wasn't it? He's taken a liking to you. Even gave

33

you the same haircut."

I say nothing.

"You don't have to speak for me to get the answer," Cutter said. "I know how you little bastards work. None of you gets food for the next three days. Only you, Elmbearn," he says, pointing at Stuard.

Stuard grins as he proudly steps up to Cutter. "Does that mean I'm your favorite?"

"That means you're my servant. If Keev gets Greenfrost, I get Elmbearn." He snarls before walking away.

I return to the room, sitting on my lower bunk, and look back when I hear an angry yelp from the corner. Wildshore gets up, wiping blood from her forehead and mouth. "I hate you," she says to Stuard. She gives me a more forgiving look before making her way to her own bunk, and I take notice of her sweaty brown hair, still long, tied in a ponytail. I guess they couldn't convince her to cut it. Brave girl.

Their is no such thing as fairness in this place. We are at the mercy of the garrison. They can do whatever they want to us. I force myself to lay down on a piece of rotting wood that barely fits my small frame. At some point during the night I can hear broken sobbing from everyone in the room, including gregarious Stuard above me. We let out a unified wail together.

I think about what I am as I fall asleep. I'm half-elven. A mutt. Mix blood. It is a bad thing to be a mutt in Scorialtt. Why? And how is it that Stuard is already declaring himself the leader of the pack?

"Our blood makes us scum," the boy across from me says as we lay shivering in the dark.

No pillows or blankets. No food. No loving embrace from Mama or Da.

34

"Bartie Greenfrost," I whisper.

"Fletcher Dooran," he says. "More human than Elf. But still just a mutt."

A mutt. We look at each other while trying to ignore the splinters in our backs. Horrible prison beds. "Just a mutt," I whisper. "Please, let this be a dream"

"No," Fletcher says, rolling over to face the wall. "This is death."

6

Dance At Fipley's

Tuesday November 27th, 2018 10:13 AM

I put on my inline skates and we head to Fipley's. Tuesday is often the day I come earlier anyway, so I figure I won't be throwing them off their schedule too much. But then I hear the music blasting from the store's outdoor speakers. Cyril is dancing for the customers again...which means he must have had some morning beer.

"You mind if I get some snacks?" Kara asks.

"Go ahead. Vincent will be excited to have someone buy something this early."

I glide ahead, preparing to stop and stand near the wall, but Cyril notices me, and shouts above the music, "hey, Tenny!"

We lock eyes just as he changes the song on the stereo. A famous eighties song begins playing, and I have to dance to it. He knows one of my weaknesses. "Ya hear that?"

I roll my eyes as he calls for Vincent to come outside. "Vinny, he's doing the dance again!"

Kara's jaw drops as she watches. "You can moonwalk?"

"Is that what it's called?" I say as I dance past her.

"You're doing it in inline skates! That's amazing, Chen."

"I can also do the swing dance, the twist, and some ballroom moves if I have a partner. I'm old, Kara," I say. "I've seen it all."

"And when do you ever have a partner?" she asks as I spin around her.

"Never. I waltz and tango with my shadow."

She giggles, and Wander gives a drooly grin in her arms. "That's funny and cute."

"Hey, Tenny, you finally got a girlfriend!" Cyril yells.

I almost fall over mid-spin. "She's not my girlfriend."

Cyril turns the music down and approaches me, smiling and pointing at Kara who is now looking well-entertained by the interlude. "Does she know how old you are? The age gap could be a real problem for some women."

"She's not my girlfriend, Cyril."

"Are you sure?   And the baby is adorable.   You a daddy already?"

"Cyril, please. Please, stop talking."

"It's okay," Kara says. She looks at Cyril. "We're not dating. He just brought me here so you guys could fix my car." She heads into the store, Vincent following, and I cringe when I hear him start asking her his own set of questions.

"Look, Tenny," Cyril says to me, "you know we all wanna see you enjoying life. I know you like your personal space. But if that woman is unattached, I'd think hard about being with her."

"No, that's not what's happening. I live alone, Cyril. I always live alone."

"She's pretty cute. She said she has car trouble?"

"Yes. Can you come with us to see what's wrong with it?"

Cyril looks me up and down. "Where's your helmet?"

"Didn't bring it this time. In a hurry."

"I'll check the car for her, Tenny." He slaps me on the shoulder. "Good job letting go of the helmet. You'll be looking normal soon."

10:46 AM

I wait for Kara outside the store, leaning against the wall warmed by pale sunlight.

"Whaddya think, buddy?" Brad walks toward me, waving a pack of cigarettes in the air. He shifts the strap of the camping tent to his other shoulder as he lights up. He smells like a fast food dumpster and his long hair is covered in mouse poop and flies. Maybe he thinks he looks like me because we both have long blond hair, but I keep a tidy appearance. I never want to live in my own filth again.

"Cigarette?"

"No, Brad," I say. "But thank you."

"Ya sure? I swear it's good. It's a good time for best friends."

I half-smile. It's the same sentence from him every time.

"All right then, buddy." He pockets the cigarettes and goes down the highway. "See ya tomorrow."

I watch him mutter to himself as he walks. I can't say that humans who talk to themselves are strange...I talk to myself too. It's how I keep myself going.

"Chen?"

I see Kara next to me with Wander on her hip, a small bag of purchased snacks in her hand.

"Ready to go?" she asks.

"Yes. I'll tell Cyril to follow us back to my cabin." I start moving in that direction, but Vincent grabs my arm.

"Hey, Chenner," he says. "You forgot something."

"What?"

He holds up a peanut bar in one hand and a plastic giraffe mask

38

in the other.

"I don't have a giraffe one yet," I say as I take them.

"Yeah. Thought you might like it. And hey, wherever you're going with Kara, be careful, okay? It's a different world beyond these quaint mountains."

"I'll see you, Vincent," I say.

He nods, offers a fist bump, and I reciprocate. "Look after yourself, Chenner."

11:21 AM

"Just needed a new battery. I won't charge you for it," Cyril says to Kara. "Is it true that you and Tenny are going on a road trip?"

"He's just helping me get home safely."

"Sweet guy, isn't he? But I have to warn you about his fear of cars. He hates being in them and hates being in any vehicle other than rolling around in his blades. Good luck with him as a passenger."

"Thanks for the warning," Kara says to Cyril, smiling in my direction. "But I'll drive slow. We'll be fine."

"I've driven with him, sweetheart. He's terrified of the freeway. I don't know what it is, but seeing all that traffic and road signage just drives him up the wall." Cyril leans over the hood of the car, obviously enjoying telling Kara all my quirks.

I don't refute anything. It's all true.

"I'll just put your bags in the car and we can go," I say.

"I already did that, Chen. You just bring what you need."

"Okay." I give myself a few minutes alone in my cabin before changing into fresh clothes and black sneakers. I bring my inline skates and plastic giraffe mask, putting them on the front seat.

"Have fun," Cyril says. He backs away from us, saluting to me like I've won an honorable award. I don't salute back. What is

39

he doing?

Kara looks at my face and at the pile of shirts in my arms. "Don't you wear anything that isn't from the eighties?"

"They're just comfortable," I say.

"Yeah. You literally mix high school dork with college bad boy, but it somehow works."

I'm wearing my favorite bomber jacket over a red and white plaid sweatshirt, and a t-shirt underneath that. The clothes I'm holding are all multi-colored. My favorite long-sleeve shirt has yellow triangles all over it.

"You can put them in the trunk. There's room."

I can't believe I'm about to ride in a car. I don't like cars. They're so closed in. Like a cage.

"Those guys aren't your friends?" Kara asks.

"They're not," I say.

"They seem like friends."

"I can't call them friends."

"Why not?"

"Friends always leave or hurt me."

"So, it's easier to call them acquaintances?"

"It is." I look back at her as she waits for me to get into the front passenger seat. "I don't have friends."

7

Road Trip

12:29 PM

It's been twenty minutes of driving and I'm feeling anxious. "Any music?" I ask her.

"Sure. Pick a song." Kara points to the phone between us. "You just scroll through and a song will play through the car speakers."

I can hear Wander babbling in her car seat. Her happy little baby noises are comforting. But I'm surrounded by my reflection in the mirrors and windows. I put on the giraffe mask, catching Kara's smirk before my eyes are hidden behind the plastic. I blindly go through music on her phone, stopping when I hear my ultimate favorite singer of all time.

"What is this?"

"Sinatra," I say. "You don't know Sinatra? It's his New York song."

"No, I do know this song, but I just forgot who sings it."

I don't think how silly I might look in my giraffe mask, hands raised in horror. "How could you forget Sinatra?"

She laughs. "Okay. What other music do you like?"

41

"Andy Williams."

"Um..."

"Andy Williams and Frank Sinatra. And sometimes eighties music. Cyril plays the best songs on the stereo."

Kara's tapping the steering wheel, body swaying to Sinatra's amazing voice. "That's it?"

"What else am I supposed to like?"

"Musicians from the last five years maybe."

I tune her out, getting into my singing groove. A new Sinatra song starts playing.

"Chen, how are you singing like that? I swear it's like I'm listening to your audition tape for a national talent show."

"I'm just singing along with the music."

"Your voice sounds exactly like Sinatra."

"Practice makes perfect, right?" I grin behind my mask.

In the midst of singing along to my favorite music, I realize I can't forget about Kara's stalker. Now that stalker is probably after me too. We have a crazy person following us. It suddenly feels like Kara's trying to distract me from my duties as a bodyguard. I need to guard these girls. I need to do what I failed to do in Scorialtt. This is redemption.

And then I say, "Kara, what's he look like?"

"Who?"

"Your stalker."

"Vincent told me in the store that you love those peanut caramel bars. You get one every day."

"Peanut bars," I say quickly. "Yes, I do."

Kara's really trying to distract me. Women are good at changing the subject when they want to avoid something. Funny thing is, most women usually bring up the disliked subject to begin with.

"So, Chen, what's up with that candy obsession?"

"Come on," I say. "What's he look like?"

She blows out a sigh. "Fine. He's got light brown eyes, orange-dyed hair, and a round face. Not super tall, but he has muscular legs."

"Thank you, Kara. That helps me. I need to be ready to protect you and Wander."

"I don't think he'll get violent if he sees me with another man."

"Half-elven."

"Yeah. Half-elven."

"You think he may have killed your husband. Do you have any proof that he is a murderer?"

"No, but he always left angry voice mails about how he was gonna take me away from Anders. He sounded high."

"Deadly," I say. "Drugs will turn any sane person into a demon."

"You know about drugs?"

"Yes. I've seen enough in my lifetime." I lift my giraffe mask to look out the window for a few minutes, doing my best to ignore my reflection. "To answer your question about my peanut bar obsession, Kara, it was the first thing I ate when I came to the United States."

"How long ago was that?"

"I was sixteen. But I couldn't tell you how I got here. I fell unconscious after they rescued me."

"Rescued you from what?"

My mouth goes dry. I can't answer without a quiver in my throat.

"Chen?"

I pull the peanut bar out of my pocket and unwrap it. "I should

43

be dead right now."

"What do you mean? What happened?"

"You won't believe me."

Kara looks from me to the road. "It has to do with your scars, doesn't it?"

"It was more than physical pain. I was broken."

She doesn't push for any more information. I can tell she's letting it sink in, trying to piece it together in her mind. Women seem to like solving things on their own.

"I'm starting to get the hint that you aren't fully human," she says.

"What's making you think that?"

"Because you're sitting in a car in broad daylight wearing a plastic giraffe mask. You're freaked out over your own reflection, but you shouldn't be. You're very good-looking."

"It's not just my physical face I don't like," I say. "It's the feeling I get underneath. The guilt for what I am and what I did to stay alive."

"We've all done bad things."

"Better that you don't know everything about me, Kara."

She smiles as she drives up to a fast food restaurant. "I like listening to you. It helps me think positive."

"I'm happy it does," I say. "What are we doing here?"

"It's a drive-thru. Want some fries?"

I study the line of cars ahead of us, giraffe mask on top of my head. "All these people like fries?"

"You don't?"

"Only fries I've had are what Vincent's brought back from his city trips. They're always soggy and cold. Absolutely disgusting."

Kara laughs. "Not when you get them fresh and hot! You've

never been in a drive-thru either, have you?"

"I haven't done a lot of things. I've been in the mountains for most of my life."

"So, you haven't seen anywhere else in the United States?"

"Only here in California. Rural California."

She firmly nods. "Fair. I'll get you some of my favorite stuff. You'll love it."

I stare out the front window at a group of teenagers biking across the street. They're shouting and laughing, having the time of their lives. I wish I could've had that. They look so carefree. All these joyous humans around me. They don't know pain.

"Here, Chen," she says. "Try this."

I bite into a fry, and it's surprisingly good. "Amazing," I say. "They really do taste better right when you buy them from a store."

"I got you a vanilla milkshake too. And chicken nuggets."

I indulge in everything Kara got for me, impressed by the quality. "I like it."

"You know," she says, "you're pretty calm for someone who hates cars so much."

I brace myself as Kara does a fast lane change, nearly spilling my milkshake. I've taken the lid off of it to see what color it is. "That's because you don't drive like Cyril. He thinks near-misses are funny when I'm yelling at him to slow down."

"You yell? You seem so soft-spoken."

"That's because most of you in this world talk as loud and fast as possible. I still can't believe how much chaos humans cause just with their mouths. Makes it hard for one to think."

She glances at me when I put my giraffe mask back on. "You're an introvert, aren't you?"

45

"I like my peace."

"A homebody."

"I speak my mind only when necessary, and most of the time it's not."

"Bet you think I talk too much."

"I would never say that."

Kara chuckles. "Sure. Wanna try some country music?"

I don't say anything as she switches the song. Not bad. I could learn to like country. But I space out, mind drifting while safe behind my mask.

"Chen?"

I don't answer her.

"Chen, you're not worrying about me and Wander, are you?"

Not yet. Not until I see the stalker for myself. At some point I fall asleep for the first time in a car, and when I feel Kara nudging me awake, she tells me we're at another fast food place. Fried chicken. Never had fried chicken. It smells good outside.

8

The Whip

Wednesday September 6th, 1933 3:05 AM

"Psst! Bartholomew!" I wake up to an empty can thrown at my head. Wildshore is looking down at me from her bunk.

"It's Bartie," I groan.

"Can you sing?"

"What?" I rub my eyes, unable to get the bleary sleepiness out of them.

"Can you sing? Like sing really loud and terribly?"

"Why?"

"Let's show these guards how bad us mutts can really be! Maybe they'll let us go if we raise a racket."

"It doesn't work that way," Stuard mumbles in the bunk above me. "Shut up, Wildshore."

"My name's Mirror! And I hate you, Stuard. You made us starve."

"I didn't do anything. Thank Bartie for getting you all in trouble."

"I like Bartie," Mirror Wildshore says.

"Me too," the other girl says from her bunk.

I see Fletcher nod at me. His friend above him keeps quiet.

"We'll make them go crazy with our noise! We have to be unruly. C'mon! You in?"

"No," I say to Mirror. I roll back over on the splintery wood and close my eyes.

"Bartie!" Again with the can at my head. "Bartie, let's wake them up! Make them not get any sleep!"

"I don't want to be bad," I say.

Everyone except me gets ready to dart out into the yard. I hear Stuard cackling as he climbs down. "I was already an orphan," he says, sounding excited about stirring up chaos. "They took nothing from me. I've got nothing to lose."

"I told the elflings about this before we were split into other blocks." Mirror peeks around the corner of the open doorway. "This whole camp is gonna get wild."

I envy her courage, but I think she's about to get us all in trouble. Big trouble. "Cutter will see you," I whisper.

"He can do what he wants. I'd rather die standing out there than in this stupid room. C'mon!"

3:28 AM

I can hear the growing noise from adjacent cell blocks, and I back away from the crowd of elflings. They chant the words: "Death by divide, together alive." The chant turns into terrible singing, singing louder and worse on purpose.

We are locked behind walls and gates. There is no way out of the prison yard. I look up to see Cutter on the roof. His rifle is aimed at one person.

"Mirror!" I shout, immediately covering my mouth in regret.

Cutter looks down at me, grins, and fires a bullet. There is a break in the commotion, and everyone scrambles, wide-eyed in their search for the next gunshot.

"Don't worry, boy," Cutter calls. "She's not dead."

Mirror struggles to stand, holding onto another girl for support as she balances on her uninjured leg. She doesn't look scared. She looks ready to cause more trouble. Another round of song.

"Line up! Line up, now!"

Whistles are blown, all of us made to wait in rows for the next command. I'm between Stuard and Fletcher.

"Which one of you started this?"

I trade looks with Fletcher and look back at the ground. I can hear his nervous breathing.

"Which one?" Cutter roars.

Mirror limps forward, exposing herself in the middle of the yard. Guards are watching us from all angles.

"No hesitation from the fiery mutt queen?"

She keeps her head down.

"You punishment is all of their punishment, Wildshore. You get the whip for this." Cutter lifts her head to look into his eyes. "And you, girl, sleep in my quarters for the next two nights."

She flinches at his rough hands, but says nothing.

"Prepare them! Every bastard in every block pays with forty lashes! Now!"

Cutter stomps past us, snorting like an angry dragon. His voice is deeper than normal. It's demonic.

4:45 AM

Rows of whipping posts line the entire yard. We were told to wait in our bunks before being led to the punishment. Now that I see what's about to happen, I feel sick. There's no way to run. No one to help us.

"All right, Bartie," Keev says. "Be tough." He forces me to face a post, loosely chaining my hands to it. "It's going to be bad. I'll try to go easy on you."

I stand there, heart racing as I look around at the other elflings about to endure the same torment. The guards are gathered around a table covered in white powder, each of them wildly inhaling it like gulping air after being under water.

"Bet I make it longer than you without screaming," Stuard says.

I turn to look at him, confused at his smile. He thinks it's a game.

"I'm scared," I whisper.

"I'm tougher than you."

Seeing his confidence terrifies me. He's my age and he acts like pain is the best thing ever.

"Bartie," he says again, "I'm tougher."

"No," I say. I tell myself to be stronger than him. "I am."

4:59 AM

"Gotta go hard. Take breaths, Bartie."

I whimper at the whip's bite. It intensifies until the burn is all over my body. I feel hot and cold.

"Harder!" Cutter yells. "The last fifteen better make them cry!"

I can feel Keev hesitate behind me.

"Hard, Keev! Break the bastard!"

My body is not used to so much abuse. So much violence. My legs give out, and I drop to the ground, hands still bound to the post in front of me.

"Get up," Keev says. "Get up now."

"I can't."

"Get. Up." He grazes my shoulder with the end of the whip. "Up!"

Tears blur my vision in the last five hits, and I hear my heart beating faster than I've ever heard it. Stuard is suffering beside me. We both keep eyes on each other, a silent competition of toughness happening between us.

But it's too much. Neither of us little elflings can avoid breaking down.

5:25 AM

"Here, Bartie." Keev kneels down and gives me two capsules, urging me to swallow them before anyone sees. "I'll clean and bandage the cuts later."

I try not to cry while he comforts me outside my cell. I'm supposed to go to work soon with everyone else. We get no rest. It hurts.

"Are you my friend, Keev?"

"I am your friend," he says.

"Do friends hurt each other?"

He sees the tears on my face and wipes them with a finger. "I refuse to die. Say it. Say it to me, Bartie."

I draw in a short breath, sobbing on the exhale. "I refuse to die."

"Good. Say it again."

"I refuse to die."

"Be tough," Keev says. "Be a tough mutt. You'll survive this."

"I refuse to die," I say. "I refuse."

9

The Hotel Stop

Tuesday November 27th, 2018 4:01 PM

The rain's started again. Another heavy rain.

"Fried chicken," Kara says as she points to the crispy meat in the box. "It's just a fast food version, but still good."

"I've never sat in a restaurant."

"Fast food places don't count as restaurants in my mind, but I guess it makes sense for you," she says.

I sip my cup of soda with the lid off, enjoying the bubbles floating around the top of the liquid. "Rain's not letting up, is it?"

"Yeah. Maybe we should go to a hotel tonight. It'd be safer to wait the rain out. Plus, I don't want to worry about car issues on the last stretch home."

Home. I think about what home must mean to Kara, and I think about what it used to mean to me. My childhood home. The terror that stole me from Mama and Da. I watch Wander banging her little plastic key toys on the table, her sweet face once in a while looking at me. This little one's so lucky. She's safe. She's in her mother's arms.

"Do you know what a genocide is?"

Kara stares at me with half a fry dangling from her mouth.

"A genocide," I repeat, and take a sip of soda.

"You mean, like, a mass murder?"

"I'm the last of my kind. The half-elvens. I survived a genocide."

"How long ago?"

"I was eight when it started."

She shakes her head. "Who would do that?"

"That's what I asked myself. It's what I still ask myself."

"I know this is going off topic, Chen, but why do you have such long hair? I love it, but most men can't grow hair like yours at your age. It's a little weird."

I crunch a piece of chicken. "It's because I'm a half-elven. My Da had the same hair. He taught me to braid it. I keep it long to make up for the time I couldn't in the prison camp."

"They made you cut it?"

"They did," I say.

4:29 PM

Kara starts to ask me another question, but I notice something unnerving. That man getting in line at the counter. Why does he look like...?

Cutter. It's Cutter. He's dressed like everyone else. Like a modern human.

Modern Cutter.

"But you're dead," I murmur. "I killed you."

"Chen, what's wrong?" Suddenly Kara gasps. "It's him. We have to go. It's him. My stalker's here."

"Cutter," I say.

"Elian. It's Elian. C'mon. Let's go."

I don't want to leave until I see his face. How is he here?

53

"Chen, what are you doing? C'mon. C'mon!"

Modern Cutter turns to look over his shoulder and slyly smiles in our direction. Pointy ears like mine. Terrifying white-blue eyes. It's him.

"No."

He goes up to the counter and talks to the cashier person. He acts normal. Blends in with this society.

"Chen, please, let's go."

I back out with Kara, refusing to lose sight of him. Kara doesn't see the person that I see. She doesn't see Cutter.

"That's not Elian," I say in the car. "It's Cutter."

"Elian's the name of my stalker. Who's Cutter?"

"One of the guards at Scorialtt."

She whips her head from me to the road. "Scor-what?"

"Scorialtt. You wouldn't know about it because it was wiped from all history books."

"By who?"

I look back out the window, forcing myself to stare at my reflection. "Humanity."

"Okay." Her voice softens. "It's okay. I'm sorry, Chehnuh."

I can see us pulling up to the hotel, and I realize it's where we are settling for the night. The rain and wind is torrential, so Kara is making a wise decision even though she doesn't believe I saw Cutter.

5:11 PM

I'm taken with the television as soon as I enter our hotel room. I'd rather not concern myself with sad, scary thoughts the rest of the night. I want to watch the channels. I don't have any channels at home.

Each time I press on the remote, a new colorful image pops up. I can sense Kara watching me. "That's just a shopping channel,

Chen. They just try to sell a bunch of junk to gullible people."

"No, no, don't change it." I grab the remote. "This is funny."

"You think holiday shopping is funny?"

"Are all channels like this?" I lean forward toward the screen, entranced by the silly movements of the people. "They just stand holding shiny things and walk around in circles?"

"That's how they show new products to viewers." Kara goes through her bag behind me. She only brought one of her big bags in from the car. "You laugh at weird things."

I don't take my eyes off the television. I feel something drop into my lap and look down.

"Try these, Chen."

"Oh!" I excitedly lift it up. "The shiny red chocolate bag. I haven't had the fancy round chocolates since Cyril brought some back from his brother's vacation house."

"Well, I've had them in my bag this whole time. Didn't plan on eating them."

I half-smile as a thank you to her, unwrapping one of the chocolates. As I toss a third one into my mouth, I look at my watch.

"Hey Kara, I need to do my workout. Do you mind?"

"No, you're good." She's holding Wander in her lap, helping her turn the pages of a softcover book. "I thought you did a workout at seven?"

"Need to do it now," I say, munching another chocolate. "Helps me stay calm."

Kara nods, briefly looking at the television screen where the funny shopping continues to roll on. "Did you ever have a girlfriend?"

"No girlfriend. But I think a girl liked me a long time ago. She was tortured too."

55

"Do you have a last name? Maybe half-elvens don't have one, but I think that all my favorite fantasy characters have a cool last name."

"My name was Bartholomew Greenfrost," I tell her. "Bartie."

"Bartie?" She smiles saying my name out loud.

"Yes. My parents named me that. The guards changed my name to Chehnuh."

"Why did you keep the new name? You could still call yourself Bartholomew."

"No," I say. "Not after that life. I'm Chehnuh."

I duck into the bathroom to switch from jeans to soft pajama pants, and come back out while pulling off my sweatshirt and t-shirt, revealing my deepest physical scar to Kara.

"This is what Cutter did to me." I point to the aged, but clearly visible lettering on my collarbone. "He carved his name into me with a knife."

"How old were you?"

"Ten." The entire left side of my body is horribly scarred. Another reason to avoid looking in the mirror.

"Why don't you have scars on the right side?"

"I don't know. They always forced me to endure the most pain on my left side." I get down into a plank position on the floor.

"Well," Kara says, "I can't lie and say that you look bad. I feel like I'm living in one of those epic fantasy shows."

"Why?"

"There's a shirtless Elf guy doing core work in my hotel room. Plus, I'm glad to know you really do have the strength to punch and kick my stalker if you have to."

I switch to push-ups. "Cutter won't be easy to pin down," I say.

"But you were a kid when he tortured you. He hasn't seen

56

you this strong. And it doesn't matter anyway. Cutter's not my stalker, Chen. It's Elian."

"That was Cutter at the fast food place," I say.

"No. You were hallucinating."

"I wasn't."

"I didn't see Cutter."

"I know. But I did."

"If he came from a historical time like you, I think he would be super old and gray."

"He wouldn't look old," I say firmly. I keep doing push-ups. "He's half-elven like me."

"A half-elven guard beat up another half-elven?"

"Yes. He fought his way up to gain respect in the garrison. He was the most violent in Scorialtt."

"But he's dead now, Chen. He's part of your past. That's it."

"No. It's not over."

Kara starts feeding Wander with a bottle, and she watches me push myself into a serious sweat. "Am I annoying you?"

"I am just a little frustrated, yes," I say.

"Sorry. I'm not saying you're crazy."

"You are."

"I'm sorry, Chen. Look, I'll just find a movie on here."

I switch to the splits and hold my position, hearing Kara's muffled laughter. I can't help but roll my eyes at her. I almost never have to roll my eyes. "You've never seen a half-elven do the splits before?"

"I'm just amazed to see any man do that. Cheez."

"My ancestors were more agile than I am. They had to be beyond agile in order to surf on war shields, jump backward onto horses, and skip up the side of mountains."

"That's not sarcasm, is it?"

"I don't do sarcasm."

"I can tell. You just described the Elves in every fantasy movie, show, and video game. Except I don't think any of them did the splits in parachute pants."

"They're just my pajamas." I switch to balancing on one leg.

"I'm sorry, Chen. I'm done laughing."

"It's fine. I'm glad I can amuse you with my workout."

But in truth, her amusement doesn't amuse me. Women seem to get really giggly and excited when they watch me do anything. Even when I'm just gliding around Fipley's in my inlines, apparently that means I'm the perfect stranger to get a picture with. On rare occasion I've had girl teenagers run to me from their cars holding their phones out like I'm a special tourist stop. None of them kinder than Elana though.

10

Frenemy

Wednesday September 6th, 1933 4:12 PM

I keep wondering why we are digging such deep, long holes. The garrison keeps a close eye on us from every corner of the camp, and their angry faces give me reason to work hard when I'm in pain. We are all in pain after the whipping.

"These are for the bad elflings. They go into the trench." Stuard's voice sounds raspy. He's telling me why we're digging, but I don't know how he read my mind.

"What does that mean?"

"We dig the graves."

"Is there any way out of here?"

"Only one way." He tilts his head toward the guards watching us. "You learn to be one of the garrison. A killer."

I turn my back at his smile.

"What are you afraid of, Bartie?" He lunges, shoving me face-first into the mud. "Fight like them."

"Fight back, Greenfrost." Cutter is standing near us, puffing a cigarette. "Stu's taken the powder. Doesn't know his own strength. Hit him back."

59

Powder? I think hard, trying to understand what Cutter is talking about. Then I remember what I saw on the table by the whipping posts. Lumps of white that looked like mashed potatoes or thick clouds.

"Listen, Bartie, and keep this in your head. Survivors don't save anyone but themselves." Stuard drops to one knee, slapping my shoulder and pressing his forehead against mine. "Forget your parents. Survive for yourself."

"How?"

"Do as I do. Befriend the guards. Become their favorite."

"I don't want to be their favorite," I say, quietly thinking of Keev who says he is my friend.

"You'll die if you don't do everything they tell you. They're training us to forget our families. They want us to become killers."

"Kill who?"

"Each other. They want us to kill each other." Stuard shoves me a second time, and this time I hit him back. We wrestle until we've fallen deep in the trench. I see nothing but Stuard's cruel, gloating grin. That's when I hear Keev's voice echoing Cutter. "Knock him out! Knock him out, Bartie!"

I look up to see the guards standing at the edge, all of them cheering for us to pummel each other.

"Tell me something, Bartie," Stuard says with an arrogant laugh, "how many punches can a soft country mutt take before passing out?"

His insult is hardly enough to make me want to hit him in the face, but instinct tells me to do it anyway. My punch loosens one of his few remaining teeth. His next punch breaks my nose.

"Stuard, c'mon! Destroy him!"

"Dodge it, Bartie! Pin him down!"

I can't think straight. My back aches from Keev's whip, and now my nose is leaking blood. I don't want to lose all of my face to Stuard. He hits me hard in the right eye, and I reel, falling backward. The trench is not wide enough to put a safe distance between us. He crawls fast, howling like a cursed wolf.

"Stuard, please! Stuard! Stop hitting me. It's Bartie. We're friends, aren't we?"

He suddenly vomits, collapsing in the mud.

"We're friends, aren't we?" I ask.

"Someone get the bastard cleaned up!" Cutter barks from outside the trench. He looks down at us, prideful eyes on Stuard. "Only Stuard gets out. You stay there, Greenfrost."

"When can I come out? I did my work."

"No." He shakes his head. "You lost the fight. If anyone helps you out of there before I do, you will pay for their disobedience."

I count ten minutes in my head after I'm left alone and see Keev above me. "Cutter never said someone can't join you, Bartie." He slides down, dirtying his clean uniform, and sits next to me. "Take this," he says, handing me an unlit cigarette.

"I don't do the smoking."

"Just try one. It'll make you feel better."

"Like the capsules?" I ask.

He chuckles and nods. "Yes. A little like that. Hold it and I'll light it for you."

I take the cigarette, fumbling to keep it in my fingers. I lift it to my mouth.

"Small, quick breaths. Hold the smoke in your mouth and let it out slowly."

I do as he says and immediately explode in a fit of coughing.

"Keep at it," Keev says. "It gets easier. Breathe out slow."

The commotion outside the trench begins to fade. I'm not

sure if an hour passes, but I smoke more. I feel dizzy, my whole face is throbbing, and Keev pushes a bottle of fire water at me. "Drink with me. Drink, little Bartie."

Between sips of fire water, I inhale smoke. I cough, vomit, and hear Keev drunkenly singing to himself...or maybe it's him singing to Scorialtt's garrison. I hear myself start to sing along. More vomit comes out. Then I see nothing and hear nothing. Nothing except the faint sizzle of my dying cigarette.

"Fire water," I mumble with my face in the dirt. "Fire water... fire capsule...fire water...fire capsule..."

9:37 PM

I'm starving at night. I have to watch Stuard eating beside Cutter while both of them oversee us mutts dig the trench even deeper. There is no light to work by and we are all tired. I was only allowed out of the trench because Cutter wanted to see me dig in the dark. My body stings from the whip and Stuard's beating. Everything hurts. I'm so hungry.

"Fallin asleep, Greenfrost!" Stuard calls out. "Work faster!"

I look at where he's standing among the guards. They're watching me struggle. Keev is laughing next to them, drinking fire water and smoking. He's coaxing Cutter to give him another piece of cooked chicken. They all eat in front of us.

"Carry the stones, bastard! Line the trench with the stones!"

Mirror Wildshore pants next to me as she tries to lift a massive rock. I trade weary looks with Fletcher Dooran. He's becoming more of a real friend to me than Stuard or Keev. All of us have to keep going or we'll die by gunfire.

"Hey, uh, Greenfrost?"

My legs are shaking as I stand the shovel upright. Cutter's breathing harshly near my ear. "How fast can you run?"

I don't speak.

"How. Fast. Can. You. Run?" He sounds drunk, unstable. "Let's have a race. You and Stuard. Each of you runs against six other mutts."

I look over at Stuard who is chewing soft bread, listening to everything.

"And then you race each other," Cutter says and spits. He wipes his sleeve across his mouth.

"It's dark," I whisper.

"More fun." He bursts out a sadistic chuckle. "More fun in the dark."

10:01 PM

It's a death trap. All of this is a death trap. Every elfling sprinting alongside Stuard is shot down. He cheats. He doesn't even lead the others in the race, and yet, he still wins. I have to race my own fellow elflings now. I don't want to do this. But I don't want to die.

"Quick as lightning, Bartie," Keev says to me. "Beat them."

I run at the whistle. I run even though I'm hungry and tired. My head aches. My back aches. But I run. I don't know if I'm winning.

"Kill the rest of them! Fire!"

I've stopped running. I'm out of breath. But dirt flies everywhere. Elflings are falling down. I'm surrounded by dead things. Dead half-elvens. Half-elvens like me. Why am I alive?

"You and Stuard, Greenfrost! Go! Go now!"

Stuard dashes in front, purposely tripping me up. I keep running. We each won our own race, and now we race each other. I grab onto his legs, madness making me wrestle him down. He gets to beat me up. I get to show him I'm strong.

"Greenfrost! Elmbearn!"

I feel a harsh light on my face as I punch Stuard. We don't stop scrambling through the mud. We don't stop hitting each other.

"Greenfrost, that's enough!"

Keev and Cutter march toward us, their breaths smelling of fire water and powder. I release my grip on Stuard, and he looks at me with a sly grin.

"Steal Cutter's cigarettes?" he asks.

"Yes," I agree.

We shake on it and stand up. Best friends. Best rivals. Nothing easy in Scorialtt. I have to make the most of my pain.

But it doesn't feel right.

Nothing feels right.

11

A Living Nightmare

Wednesday November 28th, 2018 2:07 AM

Doing my best to stay awake, slumped against the door. No voices or noises in the corridor. Kara and Wander soundly sleeping.

"Man, are you kidding me? No. I need that done by Saturday. Saturday, idiot."

I sit up straight, pressing myself to the door. That voice sounds familiar. I open the door to peer out, and see a man pacing. A man just like the one at the fast food restaurant.

Cutter.

He's on his cell phone, back turned to me. "I'm coming back Saturday. The apartment has to be ready. Yes, Kara will be with me. I love her too much to leave her behind this time." He turns around, and slows his irate rambling when he sees me.

Cutter's here. He's here to kill us.

Before I can lock the door and wake Kara, she's already sitting up in bed, rushing to pack her bag. "He's here," she says. "I know that voice."

"We should wait. He could have a gun."

"I don't wanna stay here knowing he's out there watching me. We need to go now."

I hurriedly change into my regular clothes, not thinking about Kara seeing the childish superhero boxers that Vincent had bought for me two weeks ago. "It's the middle of the night. Where are we going?"

"My friend Dakota is less than an hour from here," she says. She's breathing fast, fingers trembling as she tries to zip up the bag.

"We're not getting past him, Kara."

"We have to go. Let's go. Now."

She's bolder than I am. More foolish. I follow her as she picks up a half-asleep Wander and we all go out into the corridor where Cutter is waiting for us.

My heart thunders in my ears. She gasps.

"Where did he go?" She looks around in a panic. "Chen, where is he?"

"He's going to attack from the shadows." I'm trembling. I think I'm going to vomit. "Go, Kara. Run. Run."

"Elevator or stairs?"

"Elevator," I whisper, but rethink it as soon as we get inside and push the button. What if he's waiting for us at the bottom floor? I've never once held a baby, but I feel an urgency to help Kara move faster. "Give me Wander," I say. "Let me take her, and you get your car keys ready and run to the parking lot."

"It's fine, Chen. I got her. We're fine."

The doors open. Empty lobby.

"Go, go," I say. I don't even bother hiding my fear. We have to get out of here before Cutter comes back. He's got a gun. I know he has a gun.

"Dammit! Where are my keys?"

66

Out in the dark. He could be anywhere. He's about to attack.

"Chen, I can't find my keys. Dammit."

"We need to get out of here."

Kara sets her bag on the ground and gives Wander to me. She goes through each pocket in the bag, her search turning frantic.

"Kara. Hurry." I bounce in place like I've seen her do with Wander, trying to keep the little one calm.

There's a chill in the parking lot, a feeling of death and agony. A feeling that only a half-elven could detect. I hold Kara's baby and imagine shielding her from gunfire. What if I have to shield them both? I might. I might have to make my stand here. I have to be brave and wild.

"Yes!" Kara holds up the keys. "Let's go."

I follow her across the lot, seeing her blue car shimmering under a dim street lamp. We're almost safe again. Almost safe.

"Hi, Kara. Remember me?"

A voice in the dark.

Cutter...He's standing across from the car.

"Elian," Kara breathes out.

No. That's not Elian. I give Wander back to Kara and step in front of them. Cutter immediately sees what I'm doing. He fixates on me. "Chivalrous bastard, aren't you?"

"You've said that before." My voice sounds weak.

"Kara," he says, "your friend here is crazy. I've never said a word to him."

"Don't touch them." I stand in front of Kara and Wander and force a snarl. "Don't you touch these girls."

"All I want is my Kara back." He looks past me. "I'm not going to hurt you, baby. I just miss you."

"You're high," Kara says.

"No." He takes a cigarette from his pocket and makes a

dramatic motion as he lights it. "I'm perfectly sane. I just want to talk to you. You used to be mine."

"Did you kill Anders?"

"Why would I bother getting to your husband, babe? I can have you either way."

"Stop it!" I yell.

Cutter paces in front of Kara with an unnerving grin. "I'll give you time to think about it. When I'm ready to pick you and your baby girl up, I'll call for you to meet me. Good?"

"You're insane," she whispers.

"No," he says. "But I'd say your pal is. If he shows up instead of you, Kara, you will all pay for that mistake. I only want you and your baby when I call."

I can't see straight. Can't walk straight. Cutter's going to kill them.

"Chen, let's go. We're going to my friend's place."

Cutter backs away, watching us get into the car. His eyes don't leave mine.

"We have to keep Wander safe," I say. I sit in the backseat next to her, wanting to feel like a protector. I'm terrified. "My demons are not yet dead. Cutter's here to kill us."

"Hey. Chen." Kara reaches behind her seat to touch my hand. "It's okay. You're fine."

"He threatened you," I say. "He threatened you and Wander."

"We're going to see my friend. She'll keep us safe."

"How is Cutter here? He has a gun. And a knife. He has a knife."

"You're hallucinating, Chen."

"No. No, I'm not. He's real. He's alive."

"I'll turn some music on." Her voice and hands are shaking. She's trying to be brave but she is scared too.

I look at Wander in her car seat, happily staring back at me with her pacifier.

"Not Elian. Stalker is Cutter. He wants you dead. He wants to kill you."

"Chen, it's okay. It's gonna be fine. We're fine."

"I refuse to die," I say. I see myself in Wander's dangly mirror and shiver hard. "I refuse to die. Chehnuh refuses to die."

"Hey," Kara says. She's still reaching back to touch my hand. "You're okay. It's okay."

No.

It's not okay.

Cutter's here, Chehnuh. He's here for more blood. More violence.

You can't let him do it again.

You can't.

12

Cutter

Wednesday August 27th, 1935 1:12 PM

It's my tenth year of life. It doesn't always feel good to be smoking and drinking, but it's the only way I can stay friends with Keev and be on Cutter's good side. They target each of us without warning. We mind our own business and then one minute later...

"Greenfrost!"

I'm grabbed around the throat and carried into the torture room. I've been attacked like this before, but this time Cutter's brought his guard friends with him, and I'm thrown down on a metal table. The light is dim. All of them are drinking fire water and laughing like I'm part of a big joke.

"Make him scream," Cutter says. He backs away as I'm hit in the face by the other three guards. They pick me up and throw me to the hard floor, hurling a whip on my body.

"I didn't do anything! I promise I wasn't bad!"

"Shut up, Greenfrost. It's time you know the worth of your blood. You haven't felt pain like this, you stupid bastard mutt."

I hide my face from their blows, trying to crawl away, but they pull me back. Fire water bottles are smashed onto my legs. Glass everywhere. Shards cutting into me as I roll in it. I can't see the doorway. I can't even see the outside. I'm locked in. White powder flies in my face and I choke on it, inhaling particles. The powder that makes them crazy. The powder that's like the capsules.

"Fly high with us, mutt," Cutter says. "And it will hurt less."

"Let me go! I didn't do anything bad!"

Fire water is poured over me, and the open cuts burn. The pain intensifies. Cutter strikes me over and over with a whip. My face is bleeding, my eyes teary, I'm aggressively kicking as he sits on top of me.

"Taking the burn of alcohol and pain, Greenfrost. Strong mutt, aren't you? Strong half-breed."

"Let me go!"

"I will. But I'm finalizing your loyalty to me first. Your loyalty to Scorialtt."

The sight of his massive knife halts my screams. He isn't really going to hurt me with it. He can't. I think the worst is over, and I breathe out, blinking through the drops of sweat falling in my eyes.

"Chehnuh," he utters to me through gritted teeth. "No more Bartie Greenfrost. Chehnuh."

"Chehnuh..." I repeat.

"It means fire. You will be fire."

Cutter pushes his knife inside my body. I feel nothing but hatred stabbed into me. Pure violence. I don't know what I did to deserve this. I don't know why. It lasts for hours.

"Do what I tell you, and you will share the same privilege as Stuard. You will be my servant. Be obedient." He lays the blood-stained knife over the gaping wound he has just carved into me, snarling at my whimpers. "Do what I say, Chehnuh, and you will get food, drink, all the smokes that you crave."

"Keev," I breathe out. "I'm Keev's friend."

"You be friends with both of us. You don't know that I'm one of you, Chehnuh. I'm a mutt too." He gestures to his ears. "I escaped your fate because I am loyal to the purebloods. You be loyal to me. Understand?"

"Yes."

"Don't worry about the wound getting infected. I'll have Keev bandage it up."

There is nothing but fear as I sit up, my fingers pressed around the handle of the jagged knife. Cutter leaves it with me. Leaves me alone in the torture room.

"Bartie?" Keev comes in as the other guards exit. "Bartie, what's he done to you?"

I can barely see through my left eye. I want to vomit from the whip's burn. The entire left side of my body is on fire from their knife-slashing.

"Chehnuh." I hold my arms to my chest, rocking, shivering from the pain. "My name's Chehnuh."

13

Safe Place

Wednesday November 28th, 2018 3:20 AM

"Hey, it's Kara. Would your parents mind having me over for a couple nights? I need a place to lay low."

"The stalker again?"

"Yeah."

I rest my head against Wander's car seat, silently listening to the loud phone speaker conversation between Kara and her friend Dakota.

"I thought you went to a wedding," her friend says.

"Had car trouble. And I'm bringing a friend....an acquaintance with me."

"What friend? Is it a guy?"

"Yeah. I'll explain when I get there. Have your dad unlock the gate for me. Be there soon."

The phone clicks, and Kara looks back at me. "Dakota's parents own a ranch. She's living with them while saving up for rent. Tough to own a house or apartment in this state."

I bob my head, feeling dizzy and delirious. "I own my cabin."

"How? You don't make enough, do you?"

"No. Fipley's employees helped me out."

"That's nice of them. We're almost there, Chen."

I stare at little Wander. She's fallen asleep with her pacifier. So sweet and calm. So safe. Safe little baby. I have to keep her safe.

3:40 AM

Kara opens the door for me, and I slide out of the backseat. There's a starry-eyed, excitable young woman waiting in her robe and slippers for us. It's a dirt road. I can smell horses, sheep, cows. Country music, country ranch.

"You didn't tell me he was this cute, Kara! I could've straightened my hair."

"He's ninety-three. You're crushing on an old half-elven."

"A what?" Kara's friend asks. She studies my face. "Your eyes are ridiculous."

I frown.

"Ridiculous in a good way!" she quickly says. "I'm Dakota."

"Chehnuh."

"Take it easy," Kara says as she lifts Wander from her car seat. "He's gone through a lot of traumatic stuff."

"Well, girl, so have you! We can chill inside. There's two guest rooms."

"No room for me," I say. "I'll be on the couch."

3:52 AM

I watch Kara take Wander to bed and have a look around the front area of the house. The kitchen and living room are connected. Dakota's making a racket at the sink...apparently washing dishes while it's still dark. I start to lay down on the couch in front of the massive television, but her voice stops me.

"Want some cereal? I like eating it at night."

"Yes." I run a hand through my hair. "But only in a cup. A cup

74

with milk and cereal in it."

She gawks at me as she takes a chocolate cereal box down from the cabinet. "A cup? Really?"

"Yes."

"Huh. Maybe I should try that."

"I don't like bowls," I say.

She pours milk into a cup and lets me choose my own amount of cereal to put in. After seeing how I make my cereal, stirring it the way I like it, she gets her own cup and copies me. We sit side by side on the stools. This kitchen counter is fancier than mine.

"I can tell you're not much for sleeping. You seem restless."

"Always a lot on my mind," I say.

"So, what do half-elvens think about besides archery and talking to trees?"

"I've never done archery. I don't talk to trees either."

"What? But you have the ears and awesome hair for tree-whispering, Chen."

I dribble milk back into the cup as I respond. "How would my hair help with tree-whispering?"

"You just look like someone who loves trees. And animals." She takes another big bite of cereal, her crunching creating an echo in the silent house. "We have horses in the back. I'll show you when it's light."

"I would love to see them."

We lift our cups and sip the leftover milk at the same time. Dakota smiles at me. She looks way too awake for this time of night.

"You're lucky," I say to her. "Your parents are so kind to have you live here with them."

"I guess. Much rather be out on my own."

"It's safe here. Your family keeps you safe."

"Yeah."

"I wouldn't take that for granted, Dakota," I say. "I really wouldn't."

Family. A loving, safe family. I had that. I had everything.

11:55 AM

We take a stroll around the ranch and while walking, I can hear the girls talking about me behind my back. Kara's literally downgraded herself from a woman with a baby to a first year college student chattering away with her bestie. I don't think they realize how loud their voices are.

"He was tortured when he was little. That's why he has the scars."

"I think the scars make him look hotter."

"You can't claim him, you know, Dakota. He doesn't date."

"Are you sure? I think I could convince him."

"He had his heart broken when he was young. I think he had a girlfriend in the prison camp."

"What was her name?"

"He didn't say."

They stop gabbing the minute I decide to climb into one of the horse pens. Dakota's jaw drops as she points at me. "Tell me you're an Elf without telling me you're an Elf."

"Half-elven," Kara corrects.

"Not even my dad's best ranch guys can ride that one, Chen."

"Elf blood indeed."

I grin on top of the black-maned stallion as we run in circles. The girls are amazed. Always amazed. I like surprising them with my talents.

14

Fletcher

Friday November 29, 1935 10:14 PM

I've started sharing cigarettes with Fletcher Dooran. I learn that he's exactly fifty percent Elf and fifty percent human. A perfect mix. Stuard's been spending more time in the garrison barracks with Cutter, and sometimes he acts as a guard himself. I'm training to be a gate soldier like Keev, but I don't give up my cell block friends. Fletcher is friendlier than Stuard.

"My baby sister got killed," he says during one of our smokes.

"You saw it happen?"

He nods. "Mama was holding her."

"Want me to get us some meat?" I ask.

"Yes."

"Keev let's me eat it because I help him with the night watch."

"Did you see your parents killed?" His eyes are a stormy hue. Opposite of my bright green eyes.

"Yes." I blow out a line of smoke.

"Me too," he says. "I saw my whole family killed."

"Are you afraid of Cutter?"

"Yes."

"Me too," I say.

I don't mind his short, repetitive answers. I like sitting and hardly saying anything. "Do you drink the fire water?"

He looks sideways at me before responding. "Yes."

"Here, Fletcher." I take a bottle from behind my back and hold it out to him. He smiles. "Thanks, Bartie."

"Chehnuh," I say.

"Thanks, Chehnuh."

We take turns drinking the fire water, resting our heads against the hard wall. We should be in our bunks. But I know Keev is watching out for me. He knows where I'm at. He knows I'm with a friend. He won't let Cutter interrupt my calm moment.

"You're half-elven but you have round ears," I say.

"What of it?" Fletcher asks.

"I'm half-elven and I have pointy ears."

He stares down into the bottle and then at me. "I know."

I inhale a large cloud of smoke and start coughing, then fall over laughing. Fletcher smirks, chuckles at my strange behavior, and laughs loudly amidst flopping onto his back too.

We're flying high.

Wild-eyed.

Numb.

15

Like A Knight

Thursday November 29th, 2018 1:17 PM

The kitchen counter is crowded. Kara, Dakota, and Dakota's dad are all sitting with me while Dakota's mother serves up way too much cheesy bread.

"You don't like grilled cheese?" Dakota asks me.

"I love bread. I just don't put cheese on it."

"I feel ya, buddy," her dad says. He offers a high-five. "Cheeseless sandwich all the way."

Kara and Dakota burst into giggles when I high-five him back with a dead serious face. "Chen, you gotta work on that gesture. You're not even hitting the middle of his hand."

"I don't do much high-fiving. More fist bumps."

"So, I didn't ask you yet," Dakota says, "but what sort of car do you drive? Convertible? You look like a convertible guy."

Kara answers for me. "He prefers inline skates to walking or driving."

"Really?"

"He's good. He can dance in them."

"Why don't you skate with him, Kara?" Dakota says.

I notice Kara frowning at her.

"Yeah, Chen. She skated to all of her classes in college. In fact, I still have a pair of skates from when I tried to learn with you, Kara."

"I'm not doing that again. I haven't done it in so long."

"It's only been four years. C'mon. Show Chen. You'd look adorbs together."

I'm entertained by their conversation, and now I want to see Kara in skates. "I'll help you stay balanced."

"All right," she says. "Just don't let me fall."

2:45 PM

"Falling's part of the journey. I got you."

"Darn it! I thought it was coming back to me."

Kara holds onto my wrists as I glide backward. We're out on an empty country road. It's perfectly quiet. Calm. I've got room to do tricks on my wheels.

"You got it, you got it," I say.

She refuses to let go of me, but she's grinning as she moves forward.

"Your body's remembering it. Only been four years, right?"

"Yeah. I forgot that I even liked skating."

I half-smile. "You know how long I've been skating?"

"How long?" she asks.

"I got my first pair of roller skates when I was seventeen. I had just barely spent a year adjusting to life in this country, and someone gave them to me."

"Who did?"

"I don't know. They were just left by the door of the safe house. My name was on them."

"And you knew they would fit?"

I laugh. "It didn't matter to me. Just seemed like more fun

than walking. That was in the year of nineteen forty two. I didn't get my first inlines until nineteen eighty one."

"Wow." Kara's hands are holding mine as we continue to move down the road. She goes forward, I go backward. "You were in your fifties then."

"Yes. I found new energy. Made me laugh for the first time in a long time."

"Chen," she says, "Dakota's right about your eyes. They are ridiculous."

I tilt my head. "Ridiculous good or bad?"

"Good." She giggles. "Really, really good."

8:30 PM

The ranch house has a huge movie room that Dakota and Kara call a home theater. We're all enjoying an action-filled spectacle on the screen, and I can't get enough of fresh popcorn. I've never had popcorn before. I'm content until I notice a metallic figure in the far left corner, a figure attached to the wall near the movie screen.

"What is that?"

"That's a suit of armor my dad made for a Renaissance fair. It's super quality."

"He made it?"

"Yeah. He's good with metal."

I go toward the armor, wondering how it would fit me. Maybe I can use it as a shield if I meet Cutter again. "Would it be bulletproof?"

"I don't know." Dakota sounds distracted. She's watching the movie without a care in the world. "Parts of it probably."

"Will your father let me try it on?" I ask.

"Go ahead," she says.

I look over my shoulder at her and see her tossing popcorn

pieces into the air. I carefully disassemble the armor and start figuring out how to put it on over my clothes.

"Oh my gosh. He looks so good in that."

"Dang, Chen."

I'm backing up in front of the movie screen as I secure the bracers on my arms. Dakota, Kara, and Wander are all staring at me. It actually fits. Doesn't cover every part of my body, but it fits.

"Thank you," I say to their amazement.

Kara's phone rings, making her jump. She picks it up while watching me pace back and forth. "Hello?"

I stop moving when I see the fear in her eyes.

"Stalker," she mouths. "Elian."

Dakota puts the popcorn aside and takes Wander in her lap, turning to observe the conversation. Within five minutes the phone call ends. Kara's said nothing to him. She holds the phone tight in her hand and looks up at me. "He wants us to meet at a park on Saturday."

"Is it far?" I ask.

"No. In a neighborhood a few miles away."

"You're not going, girl," Dakota says.

I continue to pace, hearing myself clank about. "I need to confront him."

"We can just chill here. It's safer."

"The police need to get him. You said they won't arrest your stalker if he's not proven to be violent."

I see Kara and Dakota look at each other and then look at the expression on my face.

"Chen, you're not thinking..."

"I spent my youth doing everything I could to avoid death. I got other people killed because of my selfish heart. I can't do that anymore."

"You don't need to confront him. I'll tell the police to meet us there instead."

"It won't be enough. They need to see him attack an innocent person. And you are not going to be the one in front of his gun, Kara. I will."

"Don't." She stands up. "Don't you get yourself killed, Chen."

"Someone has to get him in prison. I need to do this for you."

I need to do this for me.

16

Power Hungry

Saturday August 12th, 1939 9:29 AM

On my fourteenth birthday I can see and feel my hair past my shoulders. They've let me grow it out. I do my braids again the way Da had his, but it's hard without a mirror. I still don't want a mirror. The only mirror I look at is Mirror Wildshore. She's still the bravest girl in the camp.

Mirror is always trying to get my food. I stand with the garrison, contentedly stuffing myself with bread, cheese, and chicken. The elflings are piling dirt over the dead bodies in the trench. Mirror whistles sharply before throwing a dirt clump at my head.

"Stupid guard!" she yells.

Sometimes I share food with her in secret. But I usually want all of it for myself. I don't like the empty feeling. I don't like being without my comforts.

11:01 AM

I hear Keev and Cutter arguing at the front gate. Their voices continue to get louder, more brutal toward each other. I don't understand what they're saying. One of the other guards gives me a piece of sweet bread to bite into for my birthday, but I don't swallow any of it. I hear two gunshots and Keev's voice is no longer there.

"Dead?" I stand and watch Cutter come toward me. He taps my shoulder once and keeps walking.

"Dead?" I ask again.

He turns around with a scowl. "Take your position at the gate, Chehnuh. Keev's been fired."

I let the bread in my hand drop. Stuard marches past me, rifle on his shoulder, eager to follow Cutter. "I did it," he hissed at me.

"Bastard," I whisper. I take the knife I've hidden inside my shirt and throw it at his head. "You little bastard!"

Stuard faces me. Cutter turns around and watches us glower at each other. "No mercy," he says. "Kill him, Chehnuh."

"What?" Stuard looks from him to me. Complete terror.

"Kill him, Chehnuh. Be my good servant. Kill the brat!"

I charge Stuard, but I let the knife fall. "Run!" I tell him.

He takes too long to hear me.

"Run. Run to our cell."

"And do what?" he says angrily. "You want me dead? You all want to kill me too? Do it! Do it!"

Cutter looks agitated as he puts his rifle into a firing position. Stuard doesn't move.

He's wild. He's crazy. Stuard, run.

"I've had enough of you," Cutter mutters.

He shoots.

Blood goes everywhere. Stuard's blood. All over me.

"Not quick enough, Chehnuh."

I hear my own breathing. Shallow, airless breathing.

I killed him. I got him killed.

"Back to work, boy," Cutter says. He pushes past me, and I stand without a word.

I just stand.

My friends are almost gone.

17

Night

"Chen?"

I tilt my head as I look at my reflection. Someone is next to me. A pretty girl.

"Mirror?"

"Chen? You okay?"

"Mirror," I say. "What are you doing here?"

"Chen. Chen, it's Kara. You're in the guest room. We're in Dakota's house, remember?"

"Kara, why's Mirror looking at me like that?"

"It is a mirror. You're standing in front of a mirror, Chen."

I look at Mirror who is looking back at me with a concerned expression. "It's okay, Wildshore," I tell her. "We're going to be fine."

"Chen, you're dreaming. It's just a dream."

I reach a hand out to touch her cheek, and she holds onto my fingers, pressing both of our hands against my chest. "You're pretty," I say. "I never told you that, but you're pretty."

She smiles. "Thanks, Chen. But you're just dreaming."

"No. I'm awake." I look to my right and see a bed in the room. There's a baby laying on it. "Is that your baby, Mirror?"

"Chen. Chen, wake up." She's gripping my shoulders, shaking me. "You're not with Mirror. You're with Kara. I'm Kara."

"I'm sorry I killed you," I whisper. I wrap my arms around her and I feel her rubbing my back. "I'm sorry I didn't save you," I say.

"It's okay. It's okay." She gently pushes me away, leading me into a bright area with a sink. "Chehnuh, you're okay."

I feel water dripping down my hair and my face. Water. It's cold. I'm not in Scorialtt. No water in the camp. Fire water. Where's the fire water? Mirror....she's gone. "Kara?" The woman who drives the car. Kara and Wander.

"You're okay, Chen." Kara sits me down on the bed, letting me hold tight to her hands. "You were just dreaming."

"Did I sleepwalk?"

"Yes."

"I'm sorry. I'm not used to being away from my cabin. It's a different darkness here. Can't sleep well."

"It's all right," she says. "We're safe. We're all safe here."

"What name was I saying?"

"Mirror. And then you said Wildshore."

I see the compassion in her eyes. She won't mind if I tell her. "That was the girl. She liked me in the camp. I never wanted to see her or my other friends hurt, but I was hungry. I drank and smoked. I got high on these capsules that Keev gave me." I can't stop myself from talking. I can't stop myself. "I want people to know what happened. To know what I lost. You don't know the terrors. I killed her. I killed all my friends."

"But you wanted to live, Chehnuh. You saved yourself."

"I was selfish. I wanted food."

Kara lets one of my hands go. "Only human."

"I should know better," I say with a shudder. "Half-elven. I'm part of both worlds. I didn't save them."

"I can help you get therapy."

"No." I grit my teeth and look sternly at her. "I'm made to endure this."

"I know," she says softly. "You have."

I refuse to die. "I refuse to die, Kara. I will protect you from Cutter. I will go to that park Saturday wearing the armor, and he will know my face. He won't take another good thing from this world."

She smiles, nods. I can tell she doesn't believe me. But she sits up with me through the night. We eat chocolate cereal out of a cup. Dakota joins us at the counter and changes the subject to try to make me laugh.

But I don't laugh.

I'm facing Cutter one more time.

I have to.

18

Mirror Wildshore

Wednesday December 3rd 1941 5:21 PM

"Chehnuh," Cutter says. He stands next to me as I lean against the gate. I'm chewing minty gum that he gave to me this morning.

"What are your orders?" I ask. I know when he wants something from me. Something that rewards me with extra food. I'm sixteen now, and I'm always hungry. I shake if I don't get my bread and fire water.

"In four hours, I want you to lead Wildshore outside the Scorialtt gate. She walks free."

"Why?"

"She's done enough good for me....been a great pleasure keeping me entertained in the barracks."

"And she walks free?"

Cutter pauses before saying, "I owe her that final walk. Lead her to the gate for me, Chehnuh. Understand?"

"Yes."

"Good."

I watch him turn his back and wave to his fellow guards

standing on the cell block roofs.

Mirror gets to be free. But no one here gets to be free. No elfling goes beyond the gate without a bullet in their body. I wonder for a moment if Cutter is playing a trick on us. On Mirror. But I think about warm, fresh bread. I think about perfectly charred meat. And fire water. I'm thirsty for fire water. I'm still hungry. I want my reward.

Mirror Wildshore is a good girl. Cutter won't kill her.

9:35 PM

"Mirror! Mirror, wake up." I've climbed up to her bunk and I give her shoulder a firm push. "Mirror, wake up."

"Bartie, I'm exhausted. They let us sleep early tonight. I want my sleep."

"You have to follow me," I say. "Come outside."

"Why?"

"You're leaving Scorialtt."

She takes a long time to blink and stare. "I get to go home?"

"Yes!" I climb back down, noticing the others in the room looking at us like we're crazy.

"Right now?" Mirror says.

"Yes. Yes. Right now. Come on."

Once I can sense her right behind me, I lead us into the prison yard. I expect nothing but a calm walk. Mirror grabs my hand, pulling me into an embrace as she giggles. "You're coming with me, right?"

I smile back. "I don't know. I'm just leading you to the gate."

"You're handsome in your uniform, Bartie," she says. "Even if you look like awful Cutter."

I want to tell her that Cutter is the reason she's walking to freedom. I want to tell her that he said he liked her even though she didn't like him.

91

"Mirror—" I start to say.

9:50 PM

"Aim! Aim now!"

In a split second I'm blinded by white light, Mirror looking at me in complete horror. I feel someone pulling me away from her, and I reach out, hoping she'll reach back.

"On the girl!" Cutter yells. "Fire!"

"No! No, stop!" I try hard to run forward, but I'm pinned to the ground. Mirror's looking up at the rifles. Dozens of guards. Dozens of soldiers. All of them ordered to be where I am. "Mirror..." I mouth. She is surrounded.

I watch her look over her shoulder, her terrified eyes on mine. And then they shoot.

"Mirror!"

They don't stop shooting.

"No! Cutter, no! No, No, NO!"

I feel dirt in my fingers as I clench the ground, screaming for it to end. I lay there after it's over, and I don't leave Mirror's body until they take it from my sight. She will be burned and buried. Like a captive. Like a victim. Faceless. Nameless. Forgotten.

Mirror....I killed you. I killed you, Mirror Wildshore.

I roll onto my back weeping, and stay in the yard. I stay in the yard as they yell for me to get up. Cutter is the one who grabs me by my left leg and proceeds to take me outside Scorialtt gate, dragging me the whole way.

You were right. Mirror, you were right. Awful Cutter. Awful Cutter needs to die. Don't take me like this. Don't take me like her.

19

Redemption

Modern Cutter watches me walk through the park, scowling as I approach him and his car.

"Where's Kara?"

I say nothing.

"Where's Kara, pointy ears?"

I spread my arms, letting him take in the glory of my armor.

"A show of strength to scare me off? A man dressed as an elvish knight. Kara would be one to make something like this."

"It was my idea, Cutter," I say.

"Elian. My name's Elian. Not Cutter. Where the hell is Kara? She needs to come with me right now. Her and her baby need to come with me. I've had enough of waiting. I've done everything to get her back."

"She doesn't want you."

"No? She wants you then? You don't have to get hurt, pointy ears."

"Kara is staying with her friend. She doesn't want to go with you."

"I want her." Cutter pulls out a gun from his belt. "Tell her to come here now. Right now! I'm taking my baby girl home!"

I see the same cruelty in his eyes. The same manner of violence. Cutter's high. He's going to kill Kara and Wander.

"She's not yours. You can't have her."

"I can. She's coming with me. I'm finding her and bringing her back after you're dead, freak!"

"You killed my friends, Cutter," I say. "You killed Wildshore, Keev, Stuard." I raise my voice. "You murderer! All of them!"

"I killed nobody!" he yells. "I've never hurt Kara! She's my girl! You hear me? She's mine!"

"Murderer! You killer, Cutter!" I bend forward in my throat-burning screaming, knowing what's about to happen. "You killer!"

Cutter fires the gun.

I hear bullets hit the armor, feel them rip through my skin. People are running near the park. Running away. Running toward us. Cutter runs up and smacks me across the face with his gun.

I hit the ground.

Wednesday December 3rd 1941 11:22 PM

"Show me your fight, Chehnuh. Give me a reason to spare you."

Cutter is dragging me through the mud, outside of Scorialtt. I don't want to fight anymore.

"Strike me, mutt!"

He finally lets go, and I feel his knife under my chin. "Tell me you want to live. Tell me you want to be my servant."

My vision is blurry. I can't speak without feeling sick. "Just one bullet," I say, looking up into his demonic eyes. "So many guns. Wildshore..."

He slaps me across the face. "Wildshore needed to be killed. The little slut refused to give me pleasure, and I knew her chances were spent."

"I liked her." I try to stand and fall back down on my knees. "You killed my friend. She was my friend, Cutter." My voice cracks. "Murderer."

"Come on. Strike me."

"You killed all my friends! All of them!"

"You're delirious now, Chehnuh. Fever is taking you. Strike me once and I'll give you medicine."

"Killer! My family is dead!" I lunge forward, grabbing the knife from his hand.

He spreads his arms, grinning as I plunge the short blade into his chest. I shouldn't be doing this. I shouldn't be hurting a guard of Scorialtt. But Cutter does nothing to save himself. He is evil. He is hatred.

"You killed me," he utters amidst my frenzied stabbing. "You killer, Chehnuh."

I see blood flinging from the strands of my hair. Cutter is spitting up a glob of crimson. "You killer, Chehnuh," he whispers.

I hear myself gasping for air. I drop the knife. Cutter stops talking. Stops moving. Stops breathing. I collapse next to him.

He's dead.

But I refuse to die.

Saturday December 1st, 2018 Time Unknown

"Chen!" A hoarse scream.

Sirens.

"Chen!"

Two more shots fired as Cutter stands over me.

"Drop it! Drop the weapon! Drop it now!"

95

"Chen!"

Kara. Kara's above me. "Chen, can you hear me? An ambulance is coming. We're getting you to a hospital."

"No hospital," I mumble.

"Bullets went through the armor. He didn't hit your heart or your head." She sounds surprised that he didn't aim for a kill shot.

"Angry. Wild aim. He's high. He's flying high."

"You're gonna be okay."

I raise an arm, searching for her hand, and she touches my fingers. Everything is blurry. "Take me home, Kara. Just take me home."

"Chen, you're going to the hospital."

"I don't want to go to the hospital. Take me to my cabin."

"You have bullets inside your body."

"Where's your stalker? Where is he?"

"The police have him. He's in the car."

I turn my head to look at the people and cars lined on the street. "Where?"

"He's in that police car, Chen. Right there."

I look where she points to, but the person sitting in the backseat isn't Cutter. Cutter's not there. "Where's Cutter? Cutter. Where is he?"

"It's Elian. You saved me from Elian, remember?"

I feel tears stream down my cheeks. "Elian," I say. "The man you told me about. The round face and orange hair..."

"Yeah. That's Elian. The one who's been following me." She's crying now too as she sits next to me. "Chen, it's okay. You're gonna be fine."

"I killed Cutter," I say. I remember the scene of his body in front of me. In Scorialtt. He didn't get up to hurt me again.

96

"Elian." I look toward the police car now driving away with Kara's stalker in it. Elian is the stalker. My mind is twisted. I've not seen anyone as who they really are.

"That was in the prison camp, Chen. It was a long time ago." Kara tries to comfort me by reminding me that I'm living in a different era, but her reminder doesn't help. I'm still full of shadows. I'm still full of hallucinations, nightmares, and broken dreams.

"I refuse to die." I draw in a deep breath, a searing pain in my ribs sending me into a spasm. "I refuse to die."

"Yeah." She nods, wiping her own tears. "You do."

I think about where I am. I think about Kara's baby girl. Little Wander. "Where's Wander?" I try to sit up, but the stiffness of the armor holds me back.

"It's okay. She's with my friend Dakota. Remember? You met Dakota at her family's ranch."

I panic at the rising sirens and the sight of people taking pictures with their phones. There is no place to hide. No place to evade humanity and their crazy society. "Take me home, Kara."

"I will. After the hospital, okay? I promise I'll take you home, Chen."

I close my eyes, focusing on breathing without being in pain, wanting the quiet of my cabin. The quiet of the trees. I want to be alone again. I want the peace of my old life.

20

I'm Home

Monday December 3rd, 2018 2:13 PM

I spent all of Sunday in a hospital. Not much to report from there, but I can tell you it felt like being in a echoey white cage and I didn't get to have fries or a peanut bar. But I did have some ice chips.

The drive back to the mountains has been quiet except for Kara continuing to play Sinatra music, once in awhile looking in my direction to see if I'm singing along. I don't sing. I'm tired. I'm ready to be home. We started driving at nine in the morning, and now it is two in the afternoon. My giraffe mask is sitting on top of my head.

"Two thirteen," I say as I look at my watch.

The car stops and Kara unlocks the doors. "I'll open the trunk so you can get your stuff."

I step out, but instead of going straight into my cabin, I go to the backseat. Wander looks up at me from her car seat, immediately smiling when I hold her little hand.

"Bye, baby girl," I whisper. "Grow strong like your mama."

She babbles back to me and grabs onto the dangly mirror.

"You good?"

I turn around to see Kara standing behind me, shivering in the early winter air, puffy jacket zipped up almost to her ears. She looks small. But I know she's tough.

"I am," I say.

She grabs me into a hard embrace, silent as she holds me. Silence.

Peace and silence. This is all I want.

"Goodbye, Kara."

Kara backs away and smiles into my eyes. "Goodbye...Bartie."

Bartie. She uses my birth name. "See you," I say. I wave to her and Wander as their car pulls onto the highway. They're safe for now.

I look down at my watch. I'm late for my trek to Fipley's, and can't believe that I miss it. I miss sarcastic Vincent, wacky Cyril, semi-annoying Brad. I draw in a breath before placing my things inside my cabin and putting on my inline skates. I head for the gas station, motorcycle helmet tucked under my arm, imagining what sort of greeting I'll get today. Probably the same as before. They probably didn't think much of my being gone.

"Hey, Tenny!"

The smell of tires, gasoline, old car parts.

"We got something for you," Cyril says. He and Vincent are drinking beers outside the store. No customers right now. I can hear hip-hop music behind them.

"What is it?"

"Here." Cyril throws a t-shirt at me and I catch it. "Read what it says."

I hold it up and read the words: FIPLEY'S GUY. "What's this for?"

"It's no fun without you hanging out here. Consider this your first day as our co-worker."

"What? But I've never worked at a gas station before."

"Ya kidding me, man?" Sammie Adage shouts as he exits the store, soda in hand. "With all the time you've spent eavesdropping and spinning about here in those skates, surely you know dang well what goes on at Fipley's."

"Yeah, Chenner, c'mon." Vincent comes up behind me, reaching to put a baseball cap on my head. "Drop the helmet and get to work. I'll teach ya anything you don't know before we open the tune-up shop next spring. You'll be fixing cars as good as any of us."

"Well," I say, "I get to keep wearing my skates."

"No problem, Chenner. You look good in em anyway. The girls around here think you're cute. Cute men make good business."

"Half-elven," I say.

"Yeah, yeah. Half-elven."

I shake my head with a grin as he goes into the store rambling about my good looks and how I'm their new promotional star.

"Hey, bud." Brad's approaching me with his usual cigarettes and filthy hair. "Were you on vacation? You weren't here a long time."

"I know. Had to do something important."

He looks me up and down before leaning against the wall and wordlessly offering me a cigarette. I shake my head, but join him at the wall, pulling out the two peanut bars that Kara bought for me on the drive back. I hold one out to Brad. "Want one?"

He hesitates, puffing on his cigarette, looking at me like I'm acting crazy, and then he half-smiles. He takes it. "Thanks, bud."

I nod in reply, and we both eat our peanut bars, quietly watching the cars speed down the highway.

"Hey, bud?"

"What?"

He points down at my inline skates. "Got another pair of those?"

"No."

Suddenly Cyril pops out of the store and tosses a pair of brand new skates next to me and Brad. "Here. Now you can dance all weird with Chenner." He gives a smirk and returns to the cash register.

Brad looks at me with a foolish grin and sits on the ground to put on the skates.

Cyril walks past us and changes the music to an eighties song. He does it just to see me dance.

Yes, I am quite an eccentric mountain half-elven here in the Sierras. The Fipley's crew may, in fact, be far more normal than me. But they are my friends. Today I know that I have friends. And I'm not going anywhere. I'm home.

My name is Chehnuh Bartholomew Greenfrost. I'm a survivor, a freelance bodyguard, and an inline skating Fipley's employee. Stop by sometime and say hi. I'll buy you a peanut bar.

21

Epilogue…?

Saturday December 22nd, 2018 12:19 PM

Vincent started me on the cash register last week. I'm wearing sunglasses now instead of a plastic mask. Cyril says it's progress and Vincent keeps telling me to take them off when I'm inside. But seriously, my reflection looks a thousand times better with the sunglasses. I chew gum now too. It's a spicy gum. Sort of tastes like fire water in solid form.

I glide in circles around the store shelves when I'm not forced to count cash or dance in place waiting for the card reader to work.

1:31 PM

A teenage boy enters the store and his eyes briefly shift to me before heading in the opposite direction of the register. He looks like Fletcher Dooran from Scorialtt, and he looks terribly beaten up.

I chew my gum slowly, watching him grab a peanut bar off the shelves and sit on the floor against the drink fridges. His clothing is blood-stained. Welts and knife cuts visible on his arms and face. Someone disgraced him. Someone betrayed him.

The Elf in me senses his emotional state. Lonely. Tortured. Broken.

An orphan like me. A runaway. Treated subservient by a cruel person and society. He looks so much like Fletcher Dooran.

"Hey, Chenner!" Vincent yells from the storage room. "Don't forget to unload the new boxes!"

I step out from behind the counter. "I will, Vincent!" I yell back. "Just give me five minutes."

The boy lets me approach, but frowns and clutches his peanut bar tight. He's afraid I'm going to take it or tell on him.

"Hey." I sit on the floor and take my sunglasses off. "I'm Chen," I say. "What's your name?"

He touches his broken nose and winces. He moves away.

"I'm not going to get you in trouble. What's your name?"

"Fletch," he whispers.

My stomach drops. "First or last?"

"First. Fletch Dormatt."

"Are you okay?" I ask. "Where did you come from?"

"They hurt me." He's trying to be brave. Trying to hide his pain and tears. "They hurt me at the house."

"Don't worry. I'll keep you safe."

"They'll come. They'll bring me back."

I scoot to sit beside him against the fridges, unwrapping my own peanut bar. "I'll protect you, Fletch," I say.

"Why?" he whispers back. "You don't know me."

"I know more than you think. I was an orphan once and they hurt me too. But guess what?"

"What?"

I lean in, talking as if we are part of a secret club. "They didn't keep me. I refused to die."

He says nothing more. But he nods and stays beside me.

103

Fletcher Dooran, I think. Modern Fletch. Maybe my past isn't finished with me yet.

I have a lifetime ahead of me.

Another lifetime to defend the innocent.

Better not waste it, Chehnuh.

About the Author

Han M Greenbarg has been in love with writing fiction since childhood. She is an avid coffee drinker, proud dog mom, and lover of country music and war movies. Her biggest jolts of inspiration stem from nature, a variety of film scores, and animals of all kind.